A heart divided

A heart divided

Cherie Bennett &
Jeff Gottesfeld

delacorte press

Published by
Delacorte Press
an imprint of
Random House Children's Books
a division of Random House, Inc.
New York

Visit us on the Web! www.randomhouse.com/teens
Educators and librarians, for a variety of teaching tools, visit us at www.randomhouse.com/teachers
Library of Congress Cataloging-in-Publication Data
Bennett, Cherie.
A heart divided / Cherie Bennett and Jeff Gottesfeld.
p. cm.
Summary: When sixteen-year-old Kate, an aspiring playwright, moves from New Jersey to attend high school in the South, she becomes embroiled in a controversy to remove the school's Confederate flag symbol.
ISBN 0-385-32749-8 (trade)—ISBN 0-385-90039-2 (GLB)
[1. High schools—Fiction. 2. Schools—Fiction. 3. Moving, Household—Fiction. 4. Flags—Confederate States of America—Fiction. 5. Racism—Fiction. 6. Race relations—Fiction. 7. Theater—Fiction. 8. Southern States—Fiction.]
I. Gottesfeld, Jeff. II. Title.
PZ7.B43912He 2004
[Fic]—dc21
2003010031
The text of this book is set in 11-point Palatino.
Book design by Angela Carlino
Printed in the United States of America
March 2004
10 9 8 7 6 5 4 3 2
BVG

acknowledgments

WE ARE INDEBTED to the many people who granted us interviews in the course of our research. Thanks especially to the students, faculty, and administration of Franklin High School, Franklin, Tennessee; the Williamson County (Tennessee) Public Library; the Museum of Television and Radio, Los Angeles, and the First Amendment Center, Nashville. We gained much from Tony Horwitz's *Confederates in the Attic* (New York: Pantheon, 1998). Anna Deavere Smith's plays *Fires in the Mirror* (New York: Anchor Books, 1993) and *Twilight: Los Angeles, 1992* (New York: Anchor Books, 1994) were inspirational. We thank our editor, Wendy Loggia; our publisher, Beverly Horowitz; and their team at Random House; and our agent, Laura Peterson, at Curtis Brown Ltd. Thanks also to the teens and adults who read drafts of this novel as it progressed, especially Sarah Lodge, Juliet Berman, Maia Gottesfeld, Sofya Weitz, Kat Farmer, Julia McFerrin, and secret weapons Kate Emburg and Maketa Graves. Our years in Nashville contributed immeasurably to this novel.

For Igor Sergeyev Bennett Gottesfeld

A house divided against itself cannot stand.

—ABRAHAM LINCOLN

True patriotism sometimes requires of men to act exactly contrary, at one period, to that which it does at another, and the motive that impels them—the desire to do right—is precisely the same.

—ROBERT E. LEE

Everybody's got a hungry heart.

—BRUCE SPRINGSTEEN

prologue

Our toilet broke on the day of the night that changed my life, and it nearly ruined everything.

It was the summer between fifth and sixth grade. I was turning twelve but still looked the kind of ten where old people pinch your cheeks, and if you wear a bra it's because all your friends wear one and you don't want to be the only girl in an undershirt. We lived in Englecliff, New Jersey, across the Hudson River from New York City, one of those upscale suburbs where anxious parents hire tutors for their three-year-olds to make sure they get into the right pre-school.

Fortunately, my parents weren't like that. When my

mother was pregnant with my sister, Portia, she cross-stitched a pillow for me. It reads: THE PURPOSE OF LIFE IS A LIFE OF PURPOSE. I still keep it on my bed. The day the toilet broke, I wasn't aware enough to understand that the articles she wrote for magazines like *Glamour* ("How to Fake the Perfect Tan") and *Cosmopolitan* ("Sex Secrets of the Supermodels") weren't exactly fulfilling *her* purpose . . . which was one of the reasons why she was so determined that her daughters fulfill theirs.

On the day the toilet broke, my future Life of Purpose looked murky. I was not the kind of kid who'd, say, build a scale model of the Taj Mahal from Popsicle sticks (future Frank Lloyd Wright architectural genius). Or stay up all night to chart a lunar eclipse (future Carl Sagan astrophysics genius). Or paint flowers that embraced the joy of womanhood (future Georgia O'Keeffe artistic genius). However, if concocting stories about complete strangers or dreaming about what the latest teen heartthrob looked like shirtless counted in the future-genius department, I was quite the prodigy.

My mother's theory was that if only I was exposed to enough different things, eventually my dormant Woman of Purpose would awaken. I suspected that this woman was not dormant but nonexistent, that the girl who stood in her place was a deeply ordinary person, and that the sooner my mother accepted it, the sooner she'd leave me alone and move on to my little sister.

Nothing could convince her to give up on me. She gave

me piano lessons. Ditto Russian. Photography. Ballet. We worked on a political campaign as a family. I spent successive summers at computer, astronaut, and children-of-all-nations world peace camp. All fun; all Woman of Purpose strikeouts.

My mom's latest effort had been planned for the night of the day the toilet broke. As an early birthday present, she and my dad were taking me into Manhattan to see my first "real" play. I was very excited, because *Grrl* magazine said that real plays were hip in a way that musicals, like the revival of *Grease* I'd just seen with them, were not.

My best friend, Lillith, and I devoured *Grrl*. It was *the* magazine for cool girls who shopped in vintage stores and had piercings and looked as if they did drugs and had sex even if they didn't; in other words, the kind of girls we longed to be.

Grrl decreed black the must-wear color and Decadent Diva the must-wear nail polish. So I retrieved my favorite black T-shirt from Lillith, to whom I was forever lending clothes and never asking for them back. I dug out my black pants from the floor of my closet; fortunately, they passed the sniff test. Then I uncapped my purple Decadent Diva polish and sat on my bed to paint the stubs that passed for my nails.

Add nail tech genius to the list of things that were not my future calling. I splattered Decadent Diva everywhere: cuticles, fingertips, left pants leg. There was even a Day-Glo purple splotch on my white nightstand. Only when I had finished did I recall my mom's *Seventeen* article "Manicures: Method to the Madness." Rule one: Always put down old newspaper before you polish.

My mom, though, was too busy getting dressed to notice the mess I'd made. As for my dad, he was doing something in the bathroom that was supposed to result in a functional toilet again. Periodically, I'd hear my mom shout for him to call a plumber—that we'd miss the curtain if he didn't. He'd yell back, "Just five more minutes!" Meanwhile, I was attacking my nightstand with nail polish remover, trying to think of whom I could blame for this disaster. Portia, maybe. She was barely six. She'd deny it. I'd say she was lying. She'd cry. It could work.

That's when I heard my father bellow, "Jensen!"

My mom and I both came running. Deeply disgusting flotsam gurgled out of the toilet bowl like a mini Mount Vesuvius. Already my father stood sole-deep in it. My mom couldn't resist an "I told you so" as she stormed off to call the plumber. My dad said we needed to wait for him to arrive, but my mom said they'd promised me the theater and they were taking me to the theater.

As usual, my mother won. Dad sandbagged the bathroom door with sacks of rock salt left over from the winter and arranged for the plumber to come at midnight. It would cost double, but my mom said that for me, it was worth it.

Talk about pressure.

We drove into Manhattan. My dad put the car in a lot in

the East Village. The neighborhood was *Grrl* heaven, teeming with multiple hair colors, strange tattoos, and piercings in places that had to really, really hurt. As we walked to the theater, I was lost in my own world, making up stories about the people we passed and dreaming about what various cute guys looked like shirtless.

Too soon, we traded in this wonderland for Joseph Papp's Public Theater. The performance space was puny compared to the big Broadway theaters where we'd seen so many musicals. There was no orchestra pit. In fact, there was no curtain—just a bare stage, painted black and sloping upward.

By the time we reached our seats, it was nearly eight o'clock. I looked around. Three rows in front of me, a girl who embodied hip whispered in the ear of her hot, black-clad boyfriend. First, I pictured him without his shirt. Then I invented their story. He was her best friend's boyfriend. The friend was deathly ill; the couple had come together to care for the best friend and had fallen in love. They didn't want to tell the dying friend. But their passion couldn't be denied. In fact, she'd just told him how at *that very minute* she wasn't wearing any panties.

Her eyes flicked to mine. My face burned as I ducked into my open program. *The Crucible,* by Arthur Miller. Place: Salem, Massachusetts. Time: 1692. *This production will be performed without an intermission.* I couldn't believe it. I had to sit through a play set in 1692 without an intermission? That would be fine for the gorgeous girl—she'd be in the dark with the hot guy and she wasn't wearing any panties. But for me, how boring was *that* going to be?

"I know I had mints." My mother was fishing in her overstuffed purse. "So Kate. About this play. Your father explained it to you, didn't he?"

At that moment, I spied a drop of Decadent Diva on my pants leg. I edged my program over it. "No," I said.

"Pete." Her voice was tinged with irritation. "You said you'd—"

"An unplanned plumbing problem intervened," he said good-naturedly.

My parents are an interesting couple. He's Mr. Low-Key. She's Ms. Intense. He thinks she rocks the Casbah. She thinks so, too. Even now, when I'm with her, I feel like there's something I should be doing that I'm not doing, whereas with my dad, I can just *be.*

He draped an arm around me. "It's like this, Kit-Kat. The play is about the Salem witch-hunts—when people accused of being witches were burned at the stake. But Arthur Miller meant the play as a parable about the McCarthy hearings."

Dad's the only one I still let call me Kit-Kat. "What's that?"

"A parable is . . . let's see . . . well, it's a story about one thing told to illustrate another."

"I know that, we had it in English. I meant the Mc–whatever you just said."

"McCarthy hearings," my mom said, still rummaging

in her purse. "Anti-Communist hearings conducted in the 1950s by Senator Joseph McCarthy. During the Cold War, people were so scared of— Found 'em!" She snagged a lint-covered box of Altoids, wiped it off, and popped one in her mouth.

My dad picked up where my mom left off. "If McCarthy accused you of being a Communist, even without proof, your life could be ruined. It was called blacklisting. No one would hire you. Some people committed suicide."

I was shocked. "Wait, you mean someone could just lie about you and ruin your life? But that's not fair!"

My mom nodded. "Of course it's not. A witch-hunt makes no distinction between innocence and guilt. And history just repeats itself. Some group is targeted because it's different; the accusers always believe that God is on their side. I wrote an amazing op-ed piece for the *New York Times* comparing the McCarthy era to what Arab Americans are experiencing today."

I was impressed. "I didn't know you wrote for the *Times*."

"Well, they didn't print it, but they should have. Anyway, when—"

An older woman sitting in front of us turned around. "Excuse me. I don't want to offend you, but maybe your article didn't run because it was inaccurate."

My mother got that superior look on her face that I hate. "I'm a professional journalist."

The woman shrugged. "You're not the first one to get it wrong. The Arabs are the ones vilifying *us*."

"Do you have any concept of how endemic prejudice and racism are in this country?" my mother asked coolly.

I winced. It was nothing new for my mom to engage in an ideological debate with a stranger. I'd seen it happen at the grocery checkout line, at the dry cleaner, at a dance recital. It never got any less excruciating. To distance myself from her, I focused again on my program and realized that no one I had ever seen on TV or in the movies was in this play. It was going to be a really long night.

"Kate, what did you do to your nails?"

I looked up. The dispute over, my mother was staring at my hands.

A flash of brilliance hit. "It's Lillith's," I fibbed. "She got kind of messy. Some polish spilled on my nightstand, but—"

"Shhh," a man behind us hissed, because the house-lights were dimming. Saved by the fade. My mom leaned forward, my nails temporarily forgotten, and *The Crucible* started.

Here's the gist: Abigail, a teenage girl, has an affair with John, a married man. He breaks up with her. Out of spite, she accuses his wife of being a witch. Abigail's friends get in on it and accuse other people of being witches. In the end, lots of innocent people die, and John is hanged.

Within five minutes of watching Abigail slink around the stage, I was hooked. Forget the seventeenth century.

The play felt just like today. Abigail could have been the cutest girl at Englecliff High, the one other girls imitate. Watching the story unfold live, right in front of me, gave it a kind of heat I'd never experienced watching TV or at the movies. It felt real.

At that moment, something clicked in the brain of purple-polished, underachieving, almost-twelve-year-old me. At long last, the fuse of my inner Woman of Purpose was lit. I knew instantly what I wanted to do. I wanted to be a playwright. I already loved to make up stories. But instead of playing them out in my head, I would play them out on the stage. Audiences would sit, rapt, in darkened theaters. And afterward, maybe they'd see the world a little differently, with something essential forever changed in them, just as Arthur Miller's play was changing me.

When I get impossibly mad at my mother—which still happens a lot—I try to remember how insistent she was that we go to the theater that night. Here's the truth: I didn't understand what my parents said about witch-hunts and McCarthyism and racism any more than I knew how a day that began with something as mundane as a broken toilet would end with something so profound it would change my life. Any more than I knew the terrible things that would happen to my family just a few years down the road. Or what *The Crucible* and those things could possibly have to do with each other.

But they did. They do. And this is the story.

1

My knees were scrunched to my chest, palms sweaty, stomach churning, heart pounding. Panic attack. It happened every time something I wrote was about to be performed. It was happening now.

It had been five years since my epiphany during *The Crucible.* That night, I'd fallen in love with plays the way some girls fall in love with horses or dolphins. If I could have moved a cot into the back of a theater and lived there, I would have been perfectly happy.

After I declared my goal in life, my mother immediately enrolled me in a junior writing workshop at the Public Theater. Then, to nurture my nascent muse, my parents took me to a play almost every single weekend. Since they believed that anything shocking I might see onstage could act as a catalyst for discussion about societal values in general, and our family's values in particular, we went to *everything.* The first time I actually saw a completely naked man was in a drama about gay lovers, at an off-off-Broadway loft theater in TriBeCa.

I also read every play I could get my hands on—Shakespeare, Chekhov, Lillian Hellman, August Wilson, and so many more. I'd lie in bed at night, trying to peel back layers of meaning, only to find new layers. I'd wonder if I'd ever be able to write like they did, with lives fully explored in the world of the play itself.

Now, in the Public Theater's high school playwrights' lab, I sat in the back row of the same space where I'd seen *The Crucible* and tried not to hyperventilate. My friend BB slid into the seat next to me. BB—short for Byron Bruin—lived in Harlem and went to Bronx Science. His mom was a jazz composer born in Suriname, and his father was a Swedish diplomat. In the looks department, BB got the best of both worlds.

"Deep breaths," BB instructed, taking in the sweat on my forehead. He'd seen me in this state too many times.

"I'd settle for breathing at all," I managed.

He reached into his backpack. "I know just what you need."

"I don't do drugs."

"Ow!" A sharp pain throbbed in my upper arm. "What the—"

BB held up the metal ruler he'd just thwacked against my bicep.

"Jerk!" I smacked his arm. "That *hurt*."

He smiled smugly. "But notice you're breathing almost normally. The actual pain-transmission neurons in your arm override the psychosomatic symptoms of panic," he explained. "I'm running trials for a p-chem lab."

That was just so Bronx Science.

Finally, the actors took their places; the house lights dimmed and the audience hushed. As BB gave my hand an encouraging squeeze, the stage manager read the title of my piece.

PLAYED

- a short play by Kate Pride -

At rise: The ladies' room at a hipper-than-thou club. KIM and DAWN, both sixteen, run in, breathless. They're clad in the latest everything, all the trappings of beauty without achieving it.

KIM

Oh my G—

DAWN

I saw him and I'm like, whoa—

KIM

He never brought me here. He said the cover was too high. And he brings her. *Was I okay?*

DAWN

Totally. You were all like, (blasé) *Oh, hi, Kevin.*

KIM

Like, (equally blasé) *Oh, I see you're with your new girlfriend, Mia.*

DAWN

Right, you're all like, Kevin who?

They crack up and fist-bump each other, then check themselves out in the mirror and methodically pull out an arsenal of beauty products. They primp throughout the scene, often speaking to each other's reflections. Kim checks out her rear view.

KIM

Okay, I am a total cow. You could snort lines off my ass.

DAWN

Shut up! *You are so hot.*

KIM

Hotter than—?

DAWN

Totally! Did you check out those thighs? Every time she takes a step, they like, suffocate each other.

KIM

And what is up with that do?

DAWN

Hello, *Chia Pet?*

KIM

And that uni!

DAWN

I should have been all like, Oh, cute outfit. My mother *has it.*

They crack up and trade another fist bump.

DAWN

I know people at her old school. The girl is played.

KIM

Really?

DAWN

Seriously *mattress tested.*

KIM

Well, Kevin and I never—you know—so if that's what he wants, then whatever. Because I am totally over—

They're interrupted when the girl they're dissing enters. MIA, also sixteen, is effortlessly beautiful and knows it. She joins them at the mirror, fixing her makeup.

MIA

(too cool)

Oh. Hi. Having fun?

KIM

Not really. This club is so played. There are like, twelve-year-olds here with fake ID.

MIA

Kevin and I are so into each other, we didn't notice. So, we should hang sometime. I'll call you.

KIM

I'll hold my breath.

Mia scrutinizes Kim.

MIA

(snarky) Cute outfit. My mother *has it.*

Triumphant, she exits. Kim is humiliated. A long, awkward beat as she tries to deal.

DAWN

Okay, she totally rides a broom.

KIM

At least her ass fits on one.

DAWN

Kimmy. The boy was never in your league.

KIM

Really?

DAWN

Really.

They methodically throw all their cosmetics back into their purses, cross to the door, and stop.

KIM

Dawnie. Thanks.

DAWN

For what?

KIM

The courtesy clueless. It's like she's so . . . and I'm so—

DAWN

Not. She's not.

KIM

Hot, you mean.

DAWN

She's not.

KIM

Really?

DAWN

Really.

Really, they both know this is a lie. And they both know they know. They share a final best-friend fist bump, take a deep breath, and laugh ostentatiously to ensure that anyone who sees them will think they're having a fabulous time. As they exit into the club, the lights fade.

There was huge applause as the houselights went up, and I grinned. My labmates had laughed so hard during the play that a few times the actors had to hold until the yuk-fest died down. That almost never happened, because everyone in Lab was so competitive. So I was psyched. But the opinion that mattered the most was that of Marcus Alvarez. He ran Lab. Still in his twenties, Marcus had already had two plays produced at the Public and been profiled in *Time.* I was sorta kinda crushing on him, as was pretty much everyone else in Lab, including BB. And BB was straight . . . most of the time.

Marcus bounded onto the stage, all kinetic energy in jeans, a white T-shirt, and tennis shoes. "Let's start with the text of Kate's play. Shout it out."

I frowned. Wasn't he going to say what he thought? Marcus wasn't known for being effusive with praise. But the piece had been such an obvious hit. He could have thrown me a word crumb. "Nice." Or even "Decent." But he didn't.

In the front row, Leigh Wong spoke up. "This girl runs into her ex with his new squeeze. Her best friend tries to make her feel better by putting down the new girlfriend and building up her friend. I found it rather trite."

Bitch. I slunk down a little in my seat.

"Come on, it was hilarious," BB called out.

"As a comedy sketch," Leigh said. "In real life, no one is like those girls."

"Only about half the kids I know," BB shot back. "Get a sense of humor."

"Chill, BB," Marcus said. "Everyone's opinion is valid. How about subtext? Someone else?"

"De girls talk like dey are all dat, but really dey both

feel insecure," volunteered another of my friends, Nia Vernon, in her singsongy Jamaican accent.

Marcus nodded. "So essentially they're giving a performance for each other, right?" He drifted up the center aisle toward where BB and I were sitting. "Think about it. In real life, anytime we're with another person, we're giving a performance. I'm giving one right now. So are you . . . and you . . . and you." He pointed randomly at people. "But what's behind that mask? You can't write what you don't know." His eyes flicked over the group and landed on me. "Kate Pride, what's behind your mask?"

Heat crept up my neck as Marcus pinned me with his gaze. I had no idea what he wanted me to say. Fortunately, he turned and addressed the group again. "I put that question to all of you. You want to be playwrights? Do the hard, scary work. Anything less, no matter how amusing, is just sound and fury and doesn't signify jack." He checked his watch. "Okay, we're done for tonight. Those of you in Showcase, I need a page each on your one-acts by next week." He gave us a quick wave and was out the door.

Kids gathered up their stuff, chattering about Marcus's latest flash of genius, but I just sat there. *What's behind your mask, Kate?* What had Marcus meant by that? And what did it have to do with his nonreaction to my scene?

"Up and at 'em, *chica*." BB pulled me to my feet.

"What's behind dat mask, girl?" Nia teased, joining us.

I looped my backpack over one shoulder as we headed for the exit. "Interpret what just happened," I demanded.

BB waved it off. "Marcus plays mind games. You know how he is." We pushed outside into the torpid July twilight, heat from the asphalt radiating under our feet. We stopped at Lafayette and Eighth to wait for a break in the traffic so we could cross.

"Was he saying that my scene lacked depth, or that I lack depth, or what?"

"Nah. He put you in Showcase," BB pointed out. "I'd *kill* to be in Showcase."

Showcase—Young Playwrights Showcase—was a special program at the Public Theater. Four high school playwrights were selected to work on one-acts with an elite group of actors for six months. Then, over a weekend in March, the plays would be produced at the Public. It was the biggest of big deals. Every Lab member, plus a couple hundred other people, had applied. Much to my joy—and shock—Marcus had selected me. So why was he all over my case?

When the traffic thinned, we crossed against the light and cut a speedy slalom through the river of pedestrians to the uptown subway. Tosca—I'd mentally named him years ago—was at his usual spot just outside the station. He was old, maybe seventy-five, with matted gray tufts of hair, leathery skin, and dirt ingrained in the wrinkles in his neck. His sad-eyed, scruffy mutt was tied to a fire hydrant with rope.

Most of the time, Tosca was just another street crazy who talked to himself. But when he tucked his violin under his chin to play, he was a god. Rachmaninoff, Tchaikovsky,

Paganini. His body snaked this way and that, as if the music was alive someplace deep inside of him.

Tosca was such a local fixture that most people didn't even see him anymore. If they did bother to toss some change into his violin case, they didn't stop to listen to his music. I don't know why that bothered me so much, but it did. It really did.

My friends disappeared down the station steps, but as usual, I waited until Tosca finished the piece he was playing. Then I reached into my backpack for the dog food and candy bar I'd stashed there, placed both in his open violin case, and hurried to rejoin my friends.

2

BB and Nia continued uptown; I got out at Port Authority and sprinted to the platform for the Englecliff bus. I found Lillith waiting for me, leaning against a wall, her skinny torso lost in a vintage Blondie T-shirt.

Lillith and I came into the city together pretty much every Saturday. I'd go to Lab, and she'd practice with her band in a SoHo loft. Then, she'd slink around downtown—Washington Square Park, Union Square—picking up and rejecting boys like candies in a giant Valentine box. Bite into one and it's too sticky-sweet; try another and it's too nutty. Like that.

The bus pulled up with a diesel roar; we paid our fares and slid into seats near the back. "So, today sucked," Lillith said cheerfully. "I met this guy in Tompkins Square who plays guitar in a reggae band. We made out for a while."

"And?" I prompted.

She shrugged. "White chocolate. Blond dreads and a trust fund. I swear, no one is authentic anymore."

"Excuse me, do you know what time it is?" This from the cute guy one row back, who was clearly addressing me. I told him I wasn't wearing a watch and turned back to Lillith, who gave me her patented evil eye.

"He was just trying to find an excuse to talk to you," she informed me in a whisper, curling a stick of gum into her mouth. "That totally never happens to me."

Was that true? It was weird, because until the summer before ninth grade, skinny Lillith—with her hip-before-its-time choppy blond hair and waifish looks—had been much cuter than I was. Then, suddenly, I morphed. My dark hair got thicker, my bust bigger, my legs longer. Cheekbones appeared practically overnight. I'd catch sight of myself in a mirror and wonder: Who is that girl?

Guys started asking me out. I had a new boyfriend on a weekly basis. My friends would say we made such a cute couple—until the inevitable breakup. It turned out that being a cute couple is highly overrated, unless you have more in common than raging hormones and the backseat of a car.

"So, what do you think of success?" Lillith asked, popping her gum. The bus belched from the Lincoln Tunnel and hung that sweeping left-hand turn where there's nothing in the world but Manhattan skyline.

"What? Like, existentially?"

"Suck-Sex," she overenunciated. "As a new name for the band. Whores of Babylon takes up too much space on a marquee."

I clutched her arm in excitement. "You got a gig?"

She gave me her best blank stare.

"Oh, a *theoretical* marquee."

"Hey, it's not like you've had a play produced yet," she pointed out. "Besides, in the great karmic equalizer of life, I should get famous before you do."

I raised my eyebrows. Sometimes it was hard to follow Lillith's logic.

"Only one of us turned into brunette Barbie," she explained, eyeing my chest. "And it sure as hell wasn't me."

• • •

I knew the minute I walked in the door that something weird was going on.

WEIRD THING #1: From our family room came the chipmunk sound of some faux-sexy pop singer. Which had to mean MTV. Which had to mean Portia. But it was almost ten o'clock, and Porsche wasn't allowed up past nine-thirty.

"Kate? Is that you?" my mom called. "We're in the family room."

WEIRD THING #2: My mom was watching MTV.

"Come here, Kit-Kat!" This from my dad. "We've been waiting for you."

WEIRD THING #3: Dad was with them. But he never watched television, except for the Mets, Jets, Knicks, and Rangers.

"What's up?" I asked as I swung into the room. Since they were together on the couch, I plopped down in the Barcalounger, which was . . .

WEIRD THING #4: Dad's Barca was his throne. And he wasn't in it.

Portia turned down the TV. My parents held hands and exchanged a meaningful look, which caused the worst line ever written in the history of bad plays and B movies to flash through my head:

I've got a bad feeling about this.

My sister was literally bouncing with anticipation. "Can I tell her, Dad?"

"I think I should, sweetie." My father turned to me and launched into a monologue that boiled down to this: He'd accepted an amazing job offer as a design consultant for Saturn automobiles in some town near Nashville.

"Nashville . . . Tennessee?" I ventured, hoping there was another Nashville I hadn't heard about, say between the George Washington and Tappan Zee bridges.

My father nodded.

Okay. This wasn't so bad. BB's father commuted between Manhattan and Sweden. There was a kid at my school whose father worked for Warner Brothers in Los

Angeles and flew to New York on weekends. Nashville was a lot closer than either Stockholm or L.A. "Wow, you're going to rack up the frequent flier miles," I joked.

"Nuh-uh, we're all moving!" Portia blurted out.

No. This could not be happening. Only it was happening.

To be fair, it's not like this possibility had never been mentioned. I knew corporate headhunters contacted my father from time to time, offering new career opportunities. And my parents had mentioned that accepting such an offer could entail our relocating. But that had all just been theoretical. Now it was real.

My father elaborated on The Plan. We'd be moving to Tennessee for a year. After twelve months, we'd "reassess." Whatever the hell that meant.

My gut instinct was to leap from the Barca and make them realize, by any means necessary, what they were asking of me. But experience had taught me that my parents didn't react well to tantrums. So I was careful to keep my tone steady: "This is impossible for me."

"It's Tennessee, Kit-Kat," my dad said. "Not Timbuktu."

"Dad, I made Showcase. Do you have any idea what that means? I've worked toward this for *five years.*"

"You've worked toward becoming a playwright," my mom corrected me. "And if you look at the bigger picture—"

"*You* look at the bigger picture." My voice jumped half

an octave despite my quest for self-control. "How can you do this to me?"

My mother sighed. "Lose the melodrama, Kate, please."

"No! You wanted me to find a purpose for my life? Well, I found one. You can't just rip it away from me."

My mother pinched the bridge of her nose, something she often did when she was tense. "Kate, we've been completely supportive of your interest in theater, haven't we?"

I nodded warily.

"Are you under the impression that you're the only one in this family with a dream?"

This was not going well. "No."

"Good. Because this is a dream job for your dad."

I looked at him. He sat there, eyes hopeful, while Mom fought his fight. It made my heart hurt.

"I understand your disappointment," my mom went on. "And I know that your life—all of our lives—will be somewhat different. But Vanderbilt University is in Nashville, and we can look into playwriting classes for you there. I'm still going to freelance—"

"And I'm going to get my braces off and lose ten pounds before I start at my new school," Portia put in.

"The braces stay, Porsche," my mother said. "And you're not dieting."

I persevered, suggesting every option I could think of that would result in my staying in Englecliff. No, Gramma and Grampa could not sublet their Florida condo and move in with me. No, I could not live with Lillith's family. Nor Nia's. Out of options and defeated, I sank back in my father's throne. My parents dictated what they considered to be generous terms of surrender. *If* we stayed in Tennessee for more than a year, and *if* Lillith's family would have me, *maybe* I could live with them for senior year. Which meant I'd have one last shot at Showcase.

As I trudged upstairs to my room, I thought how easy this was for them. When you're forty, a year probably seems like no time at all. But at that moment, for me, it was forever.

3

"*Our flying time to Nashville will be* approximately one hour and fifty minutes. Now sit back, relax, and enjoy the flight."

"This is so cool." Portia had her forehead pressed against the window, watching our plane cut through clouds and light. She leaned over me toward my parents, who were sitting across the aisle. "Are you looking out?"

"It's beautiful, Porsche," my mom agreed.

Portia tapped my arm. "Wanna switch seats?"

I was reading *American Theater* magazine. Or trying to. "No thanks."

Her eyebrows knit. "Are you mad that you're miserable

and I'm happy? Because it's awful when someone else is all happy for the same reason you're miserable. I could *pretend* to be miserable if you want. But frankly, you'd see right through it."

I allowed that it was okay for her to be happy, and that I was happy she was happy. Then I closed my eyes and tried to sleep. But my mind kept replaying scenes from the night before, when BB and Nia had thrown me a going-away bash. All my Lab friends had come dressed in God-awful country-western wear.

Lillith had come, too. "I'll call you every day," she vowed, hugging me so hard that the rivets on her black denim jacket—actually, *my* black denim jacket, which she'd borrowed and never returned—made impressions in my arm. "I'll get T-shirts made that say FREE KATE: THE SOUTH SUCKS. I'll wear black until you come home."

To my surprise, Marcus had showed. I'd screwed up my courage the week before and asked him to coffee after Lab. Somewhere between pouring the cream and stirring the sugar, I told him my terrible news. "I'll be back next year, though," I assured him. "And then NYU, I hope."

He sipped his black brew. "Ever think about USC?"

He meant the University of Southern California, a school I had zero interest in attending. New York University was for playwrights; USC was for television writers. It was that simple.

"Why would I go there?"

"Industry contacts. You're cute. You write hip, funny,

facile, glib, all that. You could be running your own sitcom before you're thirty."

This was like telling a girl who aspired to be Rembrandt that she was a talented little cartoonist. And he knew it. I folded my arms. "In other words, you think my work lacks depth."

"You write fast food, Kate. Your characters have the weight of cotton candy. Fun going down. But ten minutes later, you're hungry for something real."

A flush crept up my neck. "Why the hell did you put me in Showcase, then?"

"Because you have talent. Possibly a lot of talent. And for some reason, I suspect you're deep. Not that anyone would know it from your writing."

"A play can be funny and still be deep," I said defensively. "I've tried to write serious. It comes out like bad Eugene O'Neill."

"That just means you're imitating him instead of being you."

"Because I'm *funny.*"

"But not superficial. Take that as a compliment."

"Gee, thanks. I feel *so* much better."

He dug a few dollars out of his pocket. "Like I said in class, Kate, you can't write—"

"What you don't know," I finished for him. "Yoda has spoken."

He almost smiled. "Exactly. So let me ask you." He leaned toward me, eyes probing mine. "What hurts so much that the pain cuts to the bone? What makes you feel so passionate you can't even breathe?"

I sat there, feeling inadequate, exposed by questions I couldn't answer. Finally I blurted out the only thing I could think of. "I'm only sixteen."

"Yeah. I guess you are, at that." He dropped the money on the table and started to edge out of the booth. He was disappointed in me. I knew that, but I didn't know how to fix it. Before he left, he wished me luck. And then he added, "Remember, Kate: Wherever you go, there you are."

• • •

My dad, who'd come down a few weeks earlier to find us a house and start his job, met us at the way-too-clean Nashville airport. He wore a broad grin, excruciatingly new jeans, and cowboy boots. Yes. Cowboy boots. He hugged us all and kissed my mom. I don't think I'd ever seen his face shine quite that way before.

New York City summers, however oppressive, are the Ice Age compared to August in middle Tennessee. We stepped out of the main terminal into air so thick you could chew the heat and wash it down with the humidity. By the time Dad led us to a new Saturn—no shocker there—I was drenched.

Back in New Jersey, my father had made fun of country music. But now, as we headed down Interstate 65 to our new home, the radio was set to a yeehaw station. He sang along. Meaning he'd already learned the words. Okay, so my dad was having fun with his new environment. That's just the kind of guy he was. Immediately, Portia proceeded to prove the power of genetics by joining in on the repetitive, hooky chorus.

Seven heartbreak ditties later, we'd passed the Nashville city limits, skirted the community of Brentwood, and taken the exit for Redford. We'd almost rented a house in Brentwood, a town that looked pretty much like Englecliff, only with hills and more open space. In fact, my mother had flown down to approve the new place. But after she had returned to Englecliff, the owner reneged on the deal. So my father had found us a home in nearby Redford that he assured us was absolutely gorgeous.

After a short stretch of fast-food restaurants, gas stations, and car dealerships, we turned onto a wide, tree-lined boulevard. Welcome to Redford, Tennessee. Population 18,451. My new home.

As Dad negotiated Redford's negligible traffic, he launched into a history lesson. Clearly he'd been studying. He seemed to know every obscure detail about the place, especially about the Civil War's bloody Battle of Redford. We passed the municipal golf course, which Dad informed us was the old battlefield. The travelog continued as we rolled down sleepy-looking streets lined with quaint-looking shops and leafy-looking trees. Not many people were out, which was sensible considering the blast-furnace conditions. "Here we are," Dad proclaimed as he pulled into a brick-paved roundabout. "Redford courthouse square. There's the monument."

Hard to miss. A gray granite obelisk jutted skyward fifty feet from a grassy area in the center of the roundabout. I learned later that etched into the granite were the names of 3,000 Confederates and 1,800 Union men who had died in the Battle of Redford. Flanking the monument, flying high and proud, were two flags: one American, one Confederate.

"Pete. At the risk of stating the obvious, that's a Confederate flag," my mother said, obviously disgusted.

I shaded my eyes to peer up at it. "We're actually going to live in a town that flies the Confederate flag? It may as well be a swastika!"

"I didn't raise it, ladies," my father said good-naturedly.

"The South lost, right?" Portia asked.

"Shhh, not so loud," my father joked. "Some folks around here still call it the War Between the States."

No one laughed. He pulled off the square and onto a side street, where we rolled past more quaintness on parade. I couldn't believe the flag didn't bother him. Clearly, the heat had fried my liberal Democrat father's brain.

Ten minutes later, we were turning into the long driveway of a stately old home. "This is it!" my dad announced. He was grinning but also looking anxiously at my mother for her approval.

It came fast. She got out of the car and took in our new

home, which was, in a picturesque Southern sort of way, beautiful. There was a long white porch with four rocking chairs and a swing that faced the road. Blue shutters framed each window; delicate lace curtains hung behind the glass. Between the lawn and the house was a lush profusion of flowers—rosebushes, pansies, and morning glories. To one side of the detached garage, there was a patch of climbing vines, heavy with ripe tomatoes.

"Wow," my mother declared.

"You like it?" he asked.

"I love it."

"Fourteen hundred Beauregard Lane," my dad marveled. "Who'd ever think that Pete Pride would live on Beauregard Lane?"

Portia was already dancing around the porch. "It's fantastic, Daddy! It's like out of a movie or something."

I wouldn't admit it out loud, but she was right. And impressive as the exterior was, the interior was even better. Downstairs was a huge kitchen with every possible convenience, a formal living room, and dining room, and a sitting room with its original fireplace. One flight up was a pair of enormous bedrooms, each with its own bathroom.

Portia followed me up the next flight of stairs, to my new room. It was a converted attic with sloping beams, cool from its own air conditioner. Along the far wall was a pile of boxes marked with my name. There was a cozy padded window seat under the eaves, and someone—Dad?—had already made my bed. Against my pillows rested the one my mom had cross-stitched for me so many years ago: THE PURPOSE OF LIFE IS A LIFE OF PURPOSE.

"Look!" Portia cried, flinging open a door. "You have your own bathroom. We won't have to share anymore!"

Okay. The place was nice. My room was nice. Having my own bathroom was nicer than nice. That still didn't mean I wanted to be there. I eyed the boxes. Unpacking would declare a permanence I wasn't ready to embrace. So instead, I went out for a walk, to see what life looked like in a town that proudly flew a racist flag.

4

I was one of the few pedestrians strolling through downtown Redford, which made sense, since the temperature was still in the mid-nineties. At first blush, the place reminded me of a 1950s movie set. The sidewalks and streets were red brick, as were most of the buildings. There was so little traffic that I could hear the grommets on the flags by the monument clang against their poles. As I waited to cross the street, an approaching car stopped even before I set foot in the crosswalk. The driver waited patiently and tipped his baseball cap to me as I crossed.

Like *that* would ever happen in Manhattan.

On closer scrutiny, though, I saw that the wholesomeness of the square wasn't all Norman Rockwell. Sure, there was your basic town hall and courthouse, old-fashioned barbershop, five-and-dime, hardware store, small-town savings and loan, et cetera. But flanking Grover's Hardware were a skateboard shop called Outrage and a used-CD place called Coda.

Next to Redford Savings and Loan was the Pink Teacup, a cozy dessert café whose plateglass window announced that it had been in business since 1928. Tinkling bells greeted me as I pushed through the door. Everything inside was pink, including the lipstick and hair ribbon on the fifty-something lady behind the counter ("My name's Roberta, honey, but call me Birdie, everyone does").

Birdie urged me to try some "fruit tea." One sip and I was hooked—icy cold, it tasted of strawberries, peaches, and spring flowers. When Birdie learned I was new in town, she made me a present of two fresh-baked butterscotch chocolate chip cookies. "I'm famous for 'em, and you can't get 'em up north," she told me. "You come on back soon, honey, and welcome to Redford!"

Like *that* would ever happen in Manhattan.

I continued my exploration on a sugar high, passing the Revco drugstore, Jimmy Mack's meat-and-three restaurant (Yankee translation: you choose a meat or chicken and three side dishes), and the one-screen Redford Cinema. Catty-corner from the cinema was an empty storefront whose whitewash announced the opening of a new Starbucks. So, mass consumer culture was invading even this corner of America. Which meant that soon people would be able to sit on the sidewalk and sip Iced Caffè Latte while enjoying the Confederate flag snapping proudly in the breeze.

I saw a sign for the Redford library and decided to have a look inside. You can tell a lot about a place by the books—and the plays—it keeps. A block off the square, the library was housed in what looked like an old mansion. Inside, it was cool and calm. A few people read newspapers. In the children's room, the walls featured giant murals of Winnie the Pooh and the Velveteen Rabbit. Kids on little chairs were listening to a librarian read aloud. That was nice.

I went to the front desk, where an elderly, white-haired woman with porcelain skin raised friendly blue eyes to mine. "Can I help you, dear?"

"I was wondering where I would find plays."

"Theatrical plays?"

I nodded. "Shakespeare, Chekhov, Arthur Miller?"

"Well, Shakespeare, Chekhov, and such, you'll find in the third aisle. Your more modern plays—I'm afraid we don't have too many, we don't get much call for that, but I've collected some fairly recently—you'll find up those stairs and to the right, in Patricia Farrior's bedroom."

"Pardon me?"

She smiled. "Daughter of Colonel James Farrior, Army

of Tennessee. This used to be the colonel's home. It's a miracle it survived the battle. Do hold tight to the handrail on your way up, dear." She pointed to a narrow, circular iron staircase.

Colonel Farrior's daughter had not lived large. In a space a quarter of the size of my new bedroom, with a similarly sloped ceiling, there was one lonely, dusty bookshelf. It held a few rows of lonely, dusty plays. Near the wall was a single wooden table, with two ancient chairs. The air conditioning didn't work as well up here; it was easily ten degrees warmer than downstairs.

I went to the bookshelf and scanned the play titles, plucking out one of my favorites, *When You Comin' Back, Red Ryder?* Still stung by Marcus's parting comments, I reminded myself that while *Red Ryder* was a serious play, it was often laugh-out-loud funny. So why couldn't I be, too? I slid into a chair and started to read.

"Ouch! Damn!" This came from *under* the table.

I pushed away from the table and jumped just as a guy crawled out and stood up. Objective truth of his physical self: my age. Tall, loose-limbed, athletic-looking. Golden tan, ditto hair; swimming pool–blue eyes. Subjective truth of his physical self: Oh. My. Gawd.

"You startled me, and I banged my . . ." He touched his forehead.

"*I* startled *you*?"

His grin could have melted the polar ice caps. "Sorry about that."

"Is hanging out under tables a little quirk of yours?"

He looked sheepish. "I was looking for something." He dropped his "g"s on "looking" and "something" with the slightest, sweetest of drawls.

"Lose your pen?"

"Not exactly."

"What if I'd had a skirt on? A *short* skirt?"

He looked stymied for a nanosecond, then rallied. "If I picked this room to look up girls' skirts, I'd be one sorry Peeping Tom. No one ever comes up here."

Okay, that was funny. "I did," I pointed out.

He chuckled. "Yeah. I guess you did."

Heat radiated between us. Or maybe it was just the crappy air conditioning. Or both. *Red Ryder* had fallen to the floor when I'd jerked away from the table; he picked it up for me and checked out the title. "You know this play?"

"Yeah. Reminds me a little of *Bus Stop*."

"William Inge," he said as he handed me back the playbook. "*Red Ryder*'s better, though." He actually knew *Red Ryder* and *Bus Stop*? Who *was* this boy?

He shoved his hands into the pockets of his jeans. "How do you like Redford so far?" What he meant was, if you lived in Redford, I'd already know you.

"Hard to say. I've been here"—I checked my watch—"three hours and twenty-seven minutes."

"How long are you staying?"

"We moved here. From New Jersey."

"Welcome to Redford. Name's Jack."

"Kate."

"Hey, Kate from New Jersey." He held his hand out to me. I took it. I didn't let go. Neither did he. We just stood there. It was ridiculous and at the same time perfect.

"How do you know those plays?" I asked.

His eyes held mine. "How do you?"

"Jackson?"

The voice startled both of us. We let go of each other's hand and backed off a half step. A pretty girl in a red-and-white cheerleading outfit with a bare midriff and world-class red hair stood at the top of the staircase. Jack—which I now understood to be short for Jackson—looked at her blankly for a second, almost as if he'd forgotten who she was. Or maybe that was just wishful thinking on my part, the way I wanted it to be.

"Hey, Sara," he finally said. "I was talking to Kate. She just moved here."

"Nice to meet you, Kate." Sara's voice was all sweetness and light. Her eyes, however, held what Marcus called an oppositional subtext. In other words, she already hated my guts. She twirled in a circle, her little skirt swishing around her trim thighs. "What do you think, Jackson? We just got the new outfits."

"Great," he assured her.

"Everybody's waiting on you at Jimmy Mack's," she said. "After that I've got a whole list of stuff we need to get done today, so chop-chop, baby."

Chop-chop, baby?

Even as she tugged him toward the stairs, his eyes were still on me. "I'll see you soon, Kate," he said.

They were gone before I realized I still didn't know what he'd been looking for under the table. But maybe, in some cosmic way (which under ordinary circumstances I *so* don't believe in, but it was already clear to me that this was not ordinary), what he was looking for was me.

5

Long ago and far away, during my mom's let's-find-out-if-Kate-is-Rodin phase, she enrolled me in a sculpture class at the North Jersey YMCA. Other kids sculpted flowers, a human hand, a ballet dancer. I made a snake. If you took that clay-gray snake, made it a gazillion times larger, and gave it square edges, it would look just like Redford High School.

On the first day, I parked my very used Saturn (my parents felt guilty enough about the move to buy me a car) in the jammed parking lot of this giant, clay-gray snake of a school and headed toward my fate.

Two Civil War–era cannons guarded the main entrance.

Overhead, an American flag hung limp in the stillness of the late-August morning. At the base of the flagpole, about fifty kids were huddled together, holding hands. It took me a moment to figure out that they were praying. The only thing kids at Englecliff High ever prayed for was a fire drill in the middle of a math test.

Following my school map and a printout of my schedule, I reached room 114 for my first class, advanced drama. If I said I wasn't hoping to run into Jack, I'd be lying. Inside the classroom, kids milled around, noisily reconnecting after the summer. It seemed as if everyone knew everyone except me. No Jack. I slid into an empty seat near the windows. Took out a pencil just for something to do. Pushed some hair behind one ear. Fiddled with the post on one earring.

I looked around. Everyone was white except for two black kids, a girl and a guy. She had high cheekbones and the carriage of a dancer. He was all sharp angles and baggy clothes. They stood near the door, arguing. And then, almost as if I had willed it, Jack walked in. My skin tingled as he slid into an empty seat and started to chat with friends. Then, as if drawn by some magnetic force, he looked right at me. A moment later, he excused himself from his friends to cross the room.

"Hey." He squatted by my seat. "We meet again."

"Hi."

"Redford looking any better to you yet?"

Oh, yeah. "Not really."

He playfully put his hand to his heart as if wounded.

"You know, you never did tell me what you were doing under the table," I reminded him. "In the library, I mean."

The bell cut him off before he could answer. He gave me a what-can-you-do shrug and headed back to his seat as our teacher, a bony woman in her forties, shut the door. She introduced herself as Miss-not-Ms. Bright, then laughed with the class because everyone but me already knew her.

Miss Bright had very expressive hands; if you didn't know better, you'd think she'd invented a new kind of sign language. As her hands flew around, she reminded the class—and informed me—that to fulfill the requirements for advanced drama, we each had to do a minimum of fifty hours of work on the school play. "I like to think that y'all would work your little hearts out anyway," she said. "Copies of the script will be available in the library as of tomorrow." Then she went on to tell us that we'd begin by doing some sharing exercises designed to build trust in the other members of our "drama family."

All righty, then. She told us to buddy up with someone we didn't know very well. I swung toward Jack, but a short girl in a shorter skirt had already corralled him. The black girl stepped over to me. She stuck her hand out. "Nikki Roberts."

I shook it. "Kate Pride."

Miss Bright continued her instructions. We had two minutes to find out as much as we could about the other person.

Nikki laughed. "She made us do the same exercise last

year. So, you transferred here from someplace in New Jersey, right?" She knew this, she explained, because she worked part-time in the office and had put in an hour before school. I was the new student from the farthest away, except one guy from Mexico City.

I told Nikki about my family, why we'd moved to Redford, and about my playwriting. She told me Nikki was short for Nicolette (a name she loathed). The black guy in the class was her twin brother, Luke, named for their father, pastor at Columbia Pike Baptist Church. And her boyfriend, Michael, had graduated from Redford High last year; he was now a freshman at the University of Louisville.

"One minute left, people!" Miss Bright called over the buzz.

"Okay, one more thing about you and one about me," Nikki said quickly. "She'll make us stand and deliver, so be prepared."

"My best friend's name is Lillith," I said. It was the first thing that popped into my head.

"I can tie a cherry stem into a knot with my tongue."

I laughed. I liked her. We still had forty seconds. I sneaked a look at Jack; his female partner was gazing up at him as if he'd just stepped down from Mount Olympus.

"Do you know that guy?" I asked Nikki, cocking my head toward Jack.

She shot me a look. "That's a joke, right?"

"Why, who is he?"

"Royalty," she said.

"Translation?"

"That's Jack—"

Miss Bright summoned us back to our seats, and started asking people to tell the class about their partner in the exercise. Nikki was one of her victims, so everyone heard about me. She called on Jack. It turned out his partner was new, too. Her name was Pansy Clifford. She'd just moved to Redford from Memphis, where she'd been cotillion queen at her old school and competed in equestrian events with her horse, Belle.

After that, we did a few basic theater games, stuff I'd done years earlier in my first playwriting class. "Great first day, people!" Miss Bright sang out when the bell rang, clapping her hands as if we'd just given a performance. Jack left without a backward glance. I was disappointed.

"So, what's the school play going to be?" I asked Nikki as we joined the teeming masses in the hall.

"Whatever it is, Miss Bright wrote it."

I was surprised. "She's a playwright?"

Nikki hesitated. "In the sense that she writes the school play every year."

"That bad, huh?"

"Let's just say that requiring her students to work on it boosts the participation level. Catch you later."

As Nikki took off down the stairs, I was already working out a plan. Maybe Miss Bright would let me write a play instead of working on hers. I'd do what I loved to do and get credit for it at the same time.

Chemistry was next. I found the lab on my map—it was clear on the other side of the building. I wondered why Jack hadn't even looked at me before he'd left class. I wondered if he'd be in any more of my classes. I wondered why I couldn't stop wondering about him.

• • •

Lunch. I sat at the top of the football stadium bleachers, dining alfresco on M&Ms and taking in the local color.

This part of Redford High was familiar: Every group had its own turf. On the football field, jocks did wind sprints. Nearby, Jack's girlfriend, Sara, and a perfectly groomed raven-haired beauty were talking earnestly to four or five girls who looked like freshmen. Beyond the north end zone was the multipierced crowd; near the south goalposts were the Hacky-Sackers, Ultimate Frisbee types, and guitar players. The geek contingent sat on the home bench, drinking slushies from Mapco, which, I quickly learned, was the nearby gas station slash junk food emporium. I glanced directly downward. Under the bleachers, the bad bleached-blond brigade sucked their lunchtime cancer sticks.

One thing about the setting, though, was definitely not familiar: The football stadium was built directly against one of the rolling hills that characterize the topography of middle Tennessee. You could see the summit from anywhere in the stands. It was barren, save for an enormous rock slab. Painted on the slab, in huge letters, was GO REBELS! and an enormous Confederate flag. The same phrase and flag were stenciled on the gridiron.

My eyes slid back to Jack's significant other. She and her friend were now leading the younger girls across the football field. As I watched, they tore sheets of notebook paper into tiny scraps and tossed them into the air. Then they turned back to the underclass girls.

"Don't you see that litter?" I heard Sara ask. "Have some respect for your school. Don't just stand there. Pick it up!"

Immediately, the younger girls scattered and dropped to their knees in a vain effort to gather up Sara's handiwork as it flew around in the breeze.

"Hey." It was Nikki Roberts. She sat next to me. "How's it going?"

"Are you watching the Sara show?"

She pulled a PowerBar out of her backpack. "Hard to miss."

"So why are those girls picking up her garbage?"

"Sara Fife is president of Crimson Maidens."

"Which are?"

"In theory, a girls' service club," Nikki said, biting into her PowerBar. "In practice, a sorority."

"Pardon me while I barf up my sleeve."

"A rich, *white* sorority," she added.

"So they're the cool white chick clique, is that it?"

Nikki nodded. "Anyone can go to their meetings at

school, but that's basically a front. It's the whole out-of-school social thing that really makes you a Crimson Maiden. For that, you have to be asked." She nodded toward the girls on the field still attempting to gather up Sara and her friend's confetti. "What you see down there is part of the unofficial hazing. Trust me. What they do off-campus to new pledges is a whole lot worse."

I popped another M&M into my mouth. "Scary." My gaze wandered up toward Redford Hill and the big flag painted there. "But that's even scarier."

"Welcome to the South," she said.

"My friends back home will not believe this."

Nikki shrugged and took a last bite of her PowerBar. "There are just as many racists up North, you know."

"Wait. Are you defending that thing?"

"Hardly. Check it out." She handed me a flyer from her backpack about a meeting she had organized to change the school team name and emblem to something that better represented the entire community. "You should come. It's tonight at my church."

"Maybe I will." I stuck the flyer in the back pocket of my jeans. Two African American girls passing by the base of the stands scowled at us. "What's up with *that*?" I asked her.

"What do you think?" Nikki rezipped her backpack.

"Let me take a wild guess: Our skin colors don't match."

Nikki shrugged. "Some of my friends have a thing about it."

"Why would you want to be friends with them, then?"

She gave me a frosty look. "Who are you to question who my friends are? I grew up with them. I've known you for five minutes."

That what she said was true didn't make it sting any less. "Fine." I got up and started down the bleacher stairs. "Whatever."

"Look, you just have to know how it is," she said, following me. "At this school, mostly kids hang with their own."

"Then why were you just hanging with me?"

"I said *mostly.*"

We walked together to the building, where Nikki gently touched my arm. "Kate, listen. You're new. I'm trying to do you a favor. This school can be . . . " She hesitated. "Let's just say I suggest you watch your step."

I laughed. "I studied playwriting in a New York neighborhood with more drug addicts than there are people in this whole town. So pardon me if I'm not quaking in my new-girl boots."

Two white guys in varsity jackets glared at us. What fun; equal opportunity racism. Near them, I saw Jack. He was taking some books from his locker. Just a simple glance at him caused a seismic disturbance. But Jack had a girlfriend, albeit a bitchy one. And I'd had cute boyfriends before. So what was it about this boy that took my breath away?

"Gotta run, late for sociology," Nikki said, pivoting away.

"Wait one sec." I edged closer. "You were going to tell

me about him." I indicated Jack, who was now slamming his locker. Sara had materialized to take possessive hold of his arm. "What did you mean about him being royalty?"

"That's Jack Redford," she explained. "As in Redford, Tennessee." She let that sink in for a moment. "Welcome to his world, baby."

6

That night, dinner-table conversation consisted of my parents' asking Portia and me about our respective first days of school, and our monosyllabic answers. Clearly, my sister was now as unenthused about Redford as I was. But things picked up when I reported on the high school's team name and emblem.

"The team is called the Rebels, and a Confederate flag is the emblem?" The loathing in my mom's voice was visceral. "Did you know about this, Pete?"

"Sure didn't," my father said, reaching for the green beans.

I told them about Nikki's meeting later that night. My

mom was completely supportive of my attending. "And Pete? You shouldn't take this so casually," she added pointedly.

I winced. It was painful to hear her reprimand him. You'd think that after eighteen years of marriage she'd realize my father was not the human dynamo she wanted him to be.

After dinner, I did some homework, then called Lillith. But all I got was voice mail. Nikki's meeting didn't start for another hour. I couldn't motivate myself to read a play, much less write one, so I puttered around my room for a while and then went downstairs. Portia was watching TV in the family room. I settled in on the couch next to her.

"God, look how thin that girl is." My sister sighed at the blond female lead dressing for a date on some insipid sitcom. "I'm a pig compared to her."

"You're not a pig."

Portia wrapped her arms around her knees. "No one even talked to me all day, Kate. No one here likes me."

"They can't not like you, they don't even know you."

"Studies have shown that first impressions are lasting impressions."

Where did she get these things? *"Studies?"* I echoed.

"I read it in *Psychology Today.* This article said there's an invisible line between the cool kids and the dorks, and even though you can't see it, everyone knows it's there. Well, the coolest girl in my grade, Madison, decided that I'm on the wrong side of the line."

I was still marveling that a sixth grader was reading *Psychology Today.* As for this so-called cool girl, Madison, I felt like smacking her. Who was she to judge my wonderful, original, quirky little sister?

A commercial came on, and I channel-surfed—a televangelist, a former-someone-now-a-no-one hawking weight-loss products, country music videos.

"Go back to the weight-loss thingie," Portia demanded.

"It's a scam, Porsche."

"Easy for you to say." She bit at her lower lip. "Today, I answered a lot of questions in class. Everyone saw that I'm smart."

"That's good."

"No, that's bad. Madison mouthed 'Shut up' at me, and then her friends all laughed." She squeezed a pillow to her chest. "If only I could lose ten pounds. And get invisible braces. And new clothes. Cool girls here don't wear jeans to school."

Her litany of woe was getting irritating. "Go wild," I said. "Start a trend."

"You can't start a trend when you're the dork and you know it. Oh, never mind." She leaned back despondently on the couch.

I checked my watch. If I wanted to go to Nikki's meeting, I had to leave. But Portia looked like she was about to cry. "Listen, Porsche, how about if we go to the mall this weekend, and I'll help you find some cute things, okay?"

"What mall?"

"I don't know. There's got to be one around here somewhere."

"'Kay." She looked up at me. "Thanks."

Sometimes it was great being the big sister. "You're welcome."

• • •

Columbia Pike Baptist Church was on the state highway between Redford and Franklin. A white, wood-framed structure, it was tiny compared to the huge Unitarian church we'd attended in Englecliff.

Not wanting to arrive too early, I ended up arriving late; the meeting had already started. I slipped into a back pew. About twenty kids sat scattered around the church. Only a handful were white. Jack Redford wasn't one of them.

Nikki stood on the raised pulpit, addressing the group. "This town is changing, and the powers that be can't stop that."

"They're sure as hell gonna try," a handsome guy down front said.

"Then we'll just try harder," Nikki insisted. "I met with McSorley after school today—"

Derisive comments and laughter rippled through the group. Paul McSorley was the high school's principal. I'd seen him in action at a brief end-of-the-first-day assembly. He wore a short-sleeve dress shirt with a tie, had an unfortunate comb-over, and used words like "swell" and "super" a lot.

Nikki waved her hand to quiet the group down. "McSorley told me that if two-thirds of the student body signs a petition, we can vote on whether to change the team name and emblem."

"How're y'all gonna get that many signatures?" a white girl with jet-black hair and a pierced eyebrow called out. Her name was Savy. I recognized her from my American history class.

"We hit the fairness issue," was Nikki's comeback. "Tell people that signing doesn't necessarily mean they want to change things. It just means they agree that it's fair to have a vote on it."

There were murmurs around the chapel as people discussed this. Nikki waited for everyone to quiet down before she started again. "There is one more thing. McSorley gave us a deadline. Six weeks."

Everyone began talking at once. A skinny guy's angry drawl rose above the cacophony. "I'll tell y'all what this is really about. McSorley's fixing to run for town council, and he's afraid to piss off the black voters. This way he can say he gave us a chance to get up a petition and still make sure it fails."

"What did you think, he'd roll out the red carpet and invite y'all down it?" a deep voice boomed from behind me. Everyone turned; a portly, middle-aged black man in a white shirt and dark tie stood in the back of the church.

Though he wasn't very tall, his commanding presence made him seem so.

"Hey, Daddy," Nikki called. Seeing Reverend Lucas Roberts for the first time made me realize that Nikki's twin brother wasn't there.

Reverend Roberts came down the aisle. "I don't want to steal my daughter's thunder," he told us, flashing a smile that looked just like Nikki's. "So I'll say my piece and get gone. Your school principal is only the first obstacle you'll face. Victory won't be handed to you just because you're right."

"Then we'll *take it*!" a boy shouted, his fist raised. There were shouts of agreement.

"Wiser men than you have trod that path, son," Reverend Roberts advised. "And failed. Your fists will not bring them down. But if you stay strong, you can prevail. I'll let y'all get on with your meeting now."

Her father departed, and Nikki laid out a plan. She'd already created a petition. Each of us would be responsible for getting a certain number of signatures. We'd have to work at it hard. But if everyone pitched in, we could make McSorley's deadline.

There was a surge of energy in the room. That was the first time I saw Nikki in action, and she was inspirational. I felt good about myself in a way I hadn't since I'd learned we were moving to Tennessee.

That's when the idea jumped into my head. I knew I couldn't lead people like Nikki could, but maybe I could move them in another way. What if I wrote a play about

Redford High School and the Confederate flag? It would be serious, important. I'd send it to Marcus; he'd see how deep my writing could be. Plus, I'd get Miss Bright to give me credit for doing it.

Perfect.

• • •

As soon as I got home, I sat down at my computer. I got the title immediately—*Black and White and Redford All Over*—and started writing like a demon.

BLACK AND WHITE AND REDFORD ALL OVER

A new play by Kate Pride

Act I, Scene 1

AT RISE: A school dance. The students wear masks that are painted half white, half black, divided down the middle. Half the kids wear American flag T-shirts; half wear Confederate flag T-shirts.

STUDENTS

(to the audience) It's only a school dance. A dance held under our two flags.

TANYA crosses to SCOTT.

TANYA

Hi, Scott.

SCOTT

Hi, Tanya.

TANYA

Would you like to dance?

SCOTT

My parents told me that I have to do three things: get good grades, go to college and marry a white girl.

TANYA

That's a terrible thing to say! They probably fly that Confederate flag, too!

SCOTT

Hey, that flag is the symbol of our school.

TANYA

Well, that flag doesn't represent me or a lot of other people.

SCOTT

Listen, nothing personal, but what color are you, anyway?

TANYA

What difference does it make? You don't have to be like your parents, Scott. Or are you some kind of racist, too?

SCOTT

No. Yes. Maybe. I don't know!

STUDENTS

(to audience) Is it racial? Am I that kind of a person? It's only a school dance!

ALEX crosses to AMY.

ALEX

Hi, Amy. Would you like to dance?

AMY

I would, but I heard Tanya likes you.

ALEX

I don't like her. She's bi.

AMY

Oh my gosh! Who told you?

ALEX

No one told me. I've seen her parents. Her mom is black and her dad is white.

AMY

(to audience) What if he knew that I'm just as mixed as Tanya? Mixed up, I mean. About the flag.

STUDENTS

(to audience) What's so important about a flag that divides us? I just want to belong. But I keep hiding behind this mask!

After five nonstop hours, I went back to consider my brilliance.

For once, a serious play of mine didn't read like a bad version of some other writer. Instead, it was worse; trite, pedantic, and strident, with not one honest emotion.

Marcus was right; I couldn't write what I didn't know. And when it came to how people in Redford really felt about the Confederate flag, I definitely did not know. With two keystrokes I highlighted everything I'd written; with a third I deleted it. The empty screen seemed fitting: as blank as me.

7

The next morning, in jeans that according to Lillith made my butt look edible, I lolled against the wall outside Miss Bright's room, waiting for Jack. I'd timed it right. Moments later, he came down the hall, laughing with another guy. His friend was shorter, with dark hair and the muscular build of a football player. Jack's eyes lit up when he noticed me. "Hey, Kate."

"Figures, he already knows you," his friend said to me, slapping Jack on the back. "This hound dog here has cute-girl radar."

"After I introduce this guy, ignore him," Jack advised me. "Kate Pride, Chaz Martin. Chaz, meet Kate, who just moved here from up North."

"Welcome, Kate Pride." He shook my hand, then he leaned close. "Don't let his Southern manners fool you. Keep both his hands in sight at all times."

I laughed, and Jack waved him off. "You were just leaving, right, Chaz?"

"Wrong. I'm already gone," Chaz called over his shoulder as he took off down the hall.

"My best friend," Jack explained. "We go way back. So, you out here holding up the wall?"

"Actually, I was waiting for you."

He looked happy about it. "Good."

"Class starts in two minutes. Which gives you one minute to explain what you were doing under the library table the other day, and one minute to sign this."

I handed him my clipboard, and he briefly scanned the petition. "You jump right in with both feet, I see."

"I've been known to."

"It's complicated."

"The under-the-table thing, or the sign-the-petition thing?"

"Both."

"Why? Because you're Jack Redford?" I challenged. "Someone filled me in on your noble lineage."

He ran his hand through his hair. "I'm thinking of changing my name."

"To what? *Jim* Redford? What's complicated about having students vote on their own school team name?"

He hesitated, and my heart sank. No matter how beautiful he was, a racist was a racist.

"I guess I misjudged you," I said. "My mistake."

"You don't understand."

"You're right. I don't."

"Arguing about names and emblems . . . it's such a waste of time. Getting rid of that flag isn't going to change one single person's life."

"Funny. I don't think you'd feel that way if you were black."

I swept past him into the classroom. As soon as the bell rang, Miss Bright's bony hands went flying as she informed us we were going to do a cold reading of some scenes from her new play. She selected a cast of ten. They sat in a semicircle, facing the rest of us.

Her opus was called *Living in Sunshine.* A wheelchair-bound girl and an undersized guy are being bullied at school. Everyone turns against them until two popular kids come to their defense. There's a fight. However, at a peer counseling group meeting, everyone realizes that the bullies lack self-esteem because they're being abused at home. The play ends with a group monologue about how a teen's life can get dark, but inside everyone there is still a ray of sunshine.

I'm not kidding. *Living in Sunshine* was so hideous that I didn't pay any attention to the actors; Laurence Olivier would've died all over again if he'd had to deliver those lines. I shuddered to think that my attempt at *Black and White and Redford All Over* had been just as pitiful. But at least I'd had the good sense to destroy it.

When the bell rang, Jack hung back as if he wanted to talk to me. But I had nothing to say, so I headed out the door. The play sucked, Redford High sucked, and Jack Redford sucked most of all.

• • •

I *had* to get out of working on *Living in Sunshine.*

After school, I went to see Miss Bright. The faculty secretary told me I'd find her backstage in her office, where she'd be meeting with the stage manager. I felt fairly confident. I'd say some nice things about her piece, then present my plan. Surely she'd be impressed with my artistic initiative and let me work on my own play.

Suprisingly, Redford High School had a decent little theater. It seated three hundred, with a proscenium arch, orchestra pit, and even fly and wing space. I went in the back way, passing the scene and costume shops, the dressing rooms, and a small rehearsal room. I found Miss Bright's office and knocked. No answer. I put my ear to the door. Nothing.

Great. Now what? I looked around. A few shafts of light cut across the hallway, illuminating a small sign that pointed to the stage. Maybe that's where she was. As I stepped around half-painted flats and klieg lights, I heard a voice from the stage. Not Miss Bright's, however. Male.

> *". . . all your ancestors owned serfs, they owned human souls."*

I recognized the line, from Anton Chekhov's *The Cherry Orchard,* and tiptoed closer to the stage, curious to see who the actor was. If you're ahead of this part of the story—which I was not at the time—then you've already figured out that it was Jack Redford. He was performing to three hundred ghosts of assemblies past.

> *"Owning living souls, it's changed you, all of you. Don't you see? You're living on the very people you won't even allow through your own front door. We live like it's hundreds of years ago. We must start living in the present. But we cannot live in the present until we own the wrongs we did in the past, and seek redemption."*

The Cherry Orchard was written more than a century ago. I'd seen three different productions. But I'd never really understood the words—never really *felt* them—until that moment.

Now, in the movie version of my life, Jack would finish; I'd clap slowly; he'd turn, see me, and smile. Which would be followed by some variation on falling into each other's arms. What actually happened was this: As I edged toward the stage, I tripped over a stray light fixture and went sprawling, one hand splashing down into an open can of orange paint.

Jack saw me. But he didn't look happy about it. "What are you doing here?" he demanded.

"I wasn't spying on you. I didn't mean . . . Look, can you get me a towel?"

I took my hand out of the can and let the paint drip back in. He went to some metal shelving on the far wall and returned with turpentine, rags, and an empty tin bucket. Wordlessly, he tossed me a few rags, then started to wipe up orange splatters from the floor.

"Thanks for your help," I told him. But he still didn't say anything. So I answered for him in my best bass voice. "You're welcome, Kate. No problem."

More silence. He wasn't making it easy. "I was looking for Miss Bright," I explained.

"She's not here."

"Yeah, I got that." My hand finally clean, I rubbed at a paint blob sinking into the floorboards. "Look, Jack, what you did just now was so . . ." I stopped. What could I say that wouldn't sound excruciatingly trite?

He wouldn't look at me. "It wasn't meant for public consumption."

"It should have been," I said. "It was so passionate, so alive, so . . ." A thought struck me. "It was like you were talking about Redford."

Still no eye contact. He reached for a clean rag. "Maybe I was."

"Then why won't you sign Nikki's petition?"

Finally he looked at me. "Could you give it a rest, please?"

"Okay. We'll stick to Chekhov. Do you know how good you are?"

He shrugged. "That monologue could make Chaz sound great."

"Hey, it's no *Living in Sunshine.*"

He burst out laughing. I did, too. We bonded over the awfulness of our drama teacher's so-called writing. And suddenly, everything was okay. It seemed like the most natural thing in the world to sit together on the floor and talk. I asked how he got interested in theater. He said when he was in middle school, an aunt had dragged him to a Chekhov festival in Alabama. It had changed his life.

"I saw *Uncle Vanya* seven times in four days," he recalled. "Can you imagine this twelve-year-old brat, tenth row center, mouthing Vanya's lines along with him?" He winced at his own recollection.

"Hey, let's do *Vanya* instead of *Living in Sunshine.*"

"I'd love to. But most people in Redford enjoy Miss Bright's plays."

"I guess that makes you a rebel, huh?"

He looked sheepish. "I was kind of hoping that if I worked up some classic monologues, she'd let me out of doing the play this year."

I laughed. "I want out, too. That's why I was looking for her."

He wagged a finger at me. "Busted. So . . . maybe we could present some scenes, then. You know. Together."

"I'm a terrible actress," I admitted. "I'm a playwright. Well, in training, anyway. I was hoping Miss Bright would let me write my own play." I told him about my years of workshops at the Public Theater, then asked where he'd studied acting. He'd been in plays at three different theaters in Nashville. But not counting Miss Bright's classes, he hadn't studied at all. This would be his fourth year in an Angelica Bright world premiere. Unless he could get out of it.

"So I take it you're going to be a drama major next year, right? What's your first-choice school?"

He didn't answer. Instead, he got up and walked toward the footlights. I followed him to the edge of the stage, where he stared out at the empty seats. "It doesn't make any sense."

"What?"

"That I love all this so much. The scenery. The lights. The way a theater smells. When I stand up here and look out there, I feel like . . . like anything is possible. I could be anyone, do anything."

"You could."

His dubious look said he didn't necessarily agree. He sat at the lip of the stage, legs dangling into the orchestra pit, and gestured for me to join him. "When I got back from that Chekhov festival in Birmingham, I told Mrs. Augustus, the librarian—smartest person I know—that I wanted to be an actor."

"Not your parents?"

"My father's dead. And my mother . . ." He left the rest unsaid. Instead, he recounted how Mrs. Augustus had handed him Tennessee Williams's *A Streetcar Named Desire* and sent him upstairs to Patricia Farrior's room with orders not to come down until he'd read the whole thing. "When I finished that, I was to read my way through every play in the library. And after *that,* she said she'd get me more."

"Nice lady."

"The best." He scanned the empty seats, as if looking for the boy he had been. "It was like all I'd ever seen was my backyard, and she handed me a map to the world."

"Yeah," I said softly. Because that was how I felt, too.

"That same day, I ducked under the desk up there and carved my initials," he continued. "As kind of a promise to myself, I guess. To follow the map she'd given me. When we met, that's what I was looking for."

"Why?"

He ran a hand through his hair. "It doesn't matter."

"Yes," I insisted. "It does."

He studied my face a moment. "That afternoon, I found a college catalog smack in the center of my bed. From The Citadel. Courtesy of my mother."

The Citadel is a public military college in South Carolina, along the lines of West Point and Annapolis. Every male Redford had been a Citadel cadet, Jack explained, since before the Civil War. Chaz's father and grandfather had gone there, too.

I scuffed my feet against the side of the stage. "So let me take a wild guess. Their theater department is not exactly hopping."

"Good guess."

"Your mom expects you to go there, even though she knows you want to be an actor?"

He hesitated. "She doesn't know. Because I never told her." Turned out he hadn't told anyone. Not Chaz. Not even Sara.

"So . . . who knows, then?" I wondered.

"Mrs. Augustus. If she still remembers."

"Who else?"

He turned, fixing those amazing blue eyes on me. And then he said: "You."

8

Jack drove a Jeep, nothing flashy. We went to the banks of the Harpeth River, which flows south through Redford. It could have been anywhere—it didn't matter to me, as long as I was with him. We talked about everything. Except his gorgeous girlfriend. And why he wouldn't sign the petition.

Hours later, back at the school parking lot, neither of us wanted to leave. It was dark now, and cool. He put his sweater around me and we kept talking. We exchanged e-mail addresses. I told him I'd be online that night. He said he'd be online, too. We both knew what we both meant.

When I got home, my parents were cleaning up from dinner. Where had I been? Why hadn't I called? I gave an evasive apology, turned down the leftovers they'd saved for me, and headed up to my room. I logged on to my computer.

You've got mail.

IM me, I'm already on. JredfordTN.

Funny how hindsight has such perfect vision, but we're always trapped in the myopic "now." We never know how important or trivial any single moment might be in the larger scheme of our lives. What you're sure is love turns out to be less than like, what's-his-name consigned to the dustbin of your personal history.

But sometimes, what feels momentous really is just that.

Those hours with Jack were momentous. We started in a theater and ended miles apart but wholly together, instant-messaging each other late into the night. As his words appeared on the monitor, I heard his voice in my head, telling me his secrets as I told him mine. And I thought: No one has ever known me before. Not really. Not until now.

Me: We've talked about everything except the two big things.

Jack: Thing one—I'm not against voting on the flag.

Put your signature where your mouth is, then.

I know you don't understand. My mother would consider it disloyal if I signed. A slap in the face.

Thing two.

Sara and I have been together since ninth grade.

Do you love her?

I'm not sure I know what that is.

Me neither. But I know what it isn't.

I care about her.

From what you've told me, she doesn't even really know you.

Maybe because I don't let her.

Then let her. If you want her, stay with her. But if you don't . . .

Sara has our lives planned. We'll get married right after I graduate from The Citadel. I'll be an Air Force officer, then come home and oversee the family investments. We'll live happily ever after as the king and queen of Redford. And we'll have a son named Jackson.

Is that what you want?

NO.

Then don't do it.

I can't shrug off my legacy like a shirt that doesn't fit anymore.

Your legacy? Who are you, the pope?

Funny girl.

Serious girl. Figure out what you want, Jack. It's your life.

• • •

A few hours later, Jack was waiting for me outside Miss Bright's room. We chatted. And it was just so . . . *chatty.*

Meanwhile, I wanted him so much that I ached down to my split ends. But he was still with Sara. And I'm not the kind of girl who grovels. Or who violates Girl Power Rule #1: "Thou shalt not steal another girl's guy, no matter how much you loathe her."

Miss Bright had more theater games up her fluttering sleeves. We had to pretend a laugh was traveling through our body until it reached our heart, like some insane, chortling aneurysm. All during this, I felt Jack from clear across the room. Everyone had to know what was up with us; how could they not know? But when the bell rang, Sara appeared at the door to drag Jack away. And away he went. Which made him a wuss. And me a fool.

After everyone left, I approached Miss Bright about writing my own play. She said the course requirement was to work on the play, not to write one. Thinking that maybe she doubted my ability, I asked if she'd read some of the scenes I'd written in my playwriting workshop in New York. In a tone as sweet as Birdie's fruit tea, she said that Redford High School didn't offer playwriting, but if it was that important to me, she was sure there were some lovely private schools to which I could certainly transfer.

"Fine," I told her through clenched teeth. "I'll work on your play."

"It's not exactly a punishment, Kate."

"I'm going to write my own, too. You can't stop me."

"I have no reason to try." She gathered up her things. "But you might want to work on your hostility issues."

At lunchtime, I was still fuming—it was easier to obsess about Miss Bright than about Jack. I met Nikki at the football field, and we went from group to group looking for signatures. She was in a great mood because her boyfriend was driving down for the weekend.

"What's he studying?" I asked as we headed for the Hacky-Sackers.

"Psych. He's pretty sure he wants to be a child psychologist. On the other hand, he thinks we should take a year off and hitchhike around Europe together."

"Do you want to?"

"Oh, yeah." She smiled wickedly, then glanced down at her clipboard. "Sometimes I just get so sick of this flag thing. Like, so what? What am I trying to prove? What different does it make, really?"

"It's made a difference to me." I admitted that she'd inspired me to write a play.

"About what?"

"The flag controversy."

"Oh, really?" She cut a glance at me as we headed for the group of kids eating under the goalpost. "You've been in Redford, what, a few weeks? And you're ready to write a play about us? Girl, you don't know a thing about it."

"You're right," I admitted. "I'm on a learning curve."

"You have no idea what you're getting yourself into."

"I'll risk it," I said dryly. "So who should I talk to?"

She thought a moment. "Mrs. Augustus, at the library. And my father."

• • •

I couldn't stop thinking about him.

Friday night, I called Lillith to give her the blow-by-blow of my lack of relationship with Jack. She said that Sara Fife fell under the Sorority Queen Exception to Girl Power Rule #1, and I should go for it. But between pride and ethics, I couldn't. And I didn't.

Saturday morning, I called Mrs. Augustus and asked if I could interview her for a writing project. She said yes, but she and her husband were going down to Tuscaloosa to visit family, so could we set it up when she returned? Then I took Portia to the CoolSprings Galleria. As she tried on clothes that Madison the Cool would deem acceptable, I wondered: What is Jack doing right now? When we stopped to buy earrings, I thought: Is he with Sara right now? I'd catch a glimpse of broad shoulders and golden hair and think: It's him. Or I'd see red hair tossed saucily down a slender back: It's her.

And then, as if thinking about something awful could actually make it happen, it really *was* them, walking toward me.

Screw him. I went directly to Sara, opening my purse as I did. "Hi." I took out one of Nikki's petitions and offered it to her. "Would you like to sign the petition to vote on the school emblem?"

"I don't think so," Sara drawled. She gave me a friendly smile and snuggled against Jack.

"What about you, Jack?" I challenged.

"Please," Sara scoffed on his behalf.

"I can answer for myself, Sara," Jack said. There was a tic in his jaw.

She kissed his cheek. "I'm sorry, baby. It's just that I've got a big ol' list of stuff we need to get done for the Crimson Maidens car wash tomorrow."

"Gee, sorry I interrupted with my silly civil rights thingie," I said.

She sighed. "Can we just go, Jackson?"

"I need to talk to Kate for a minute."

"Fine." A one-syllable icicle. She told Jack she'd meet him at the food court and left.

"Kate—"

"There's nothing to talk about. You've got exactly the girl you deserve."

"Can't we just—"

"Better go. She's got *a list*," I sneered. "You might want to add *backbone* to yours." I backed away from him and into TCBY just as Portia turned away from the counter with two cones. She handed me one. I took it and checked as nonchalantly as I could to see if Jack was still outside. He was gone.

• • •

Sunday. I couldn't think of a reason to get out of bed. My room was a mess, clothes everywhere. It was pathetic. *I* was pathetic, mourning a relationship that never was. The hell with Jack Redford, I told myself. What kind of guy stays with a girl he doesn't love? What kind of guy can't tell his own mother what he wants to do with his life? And what kind of a weenie was I turning into, lying around my room, mooning over him instead of spending time with someone I actually respected, like Nikki? Or working on my play? Or—

Pound-pound-pound on my door, followed by Portia bursting into my room and catapulting herself onto the bed. "The cutest boy is downstairs waiting for you," she announced breathlessly.

Possibly I was dreaming. Caution was key. "What color hair?"

"Goldish, kinda. Blue eyes. He told me to give you this." She handed me a piece of folded notebook paper. I unfolded a really bad drawing of something long and thin and bumpy. The caption: JACK'S BACKBONE.

"Porsche, I *love* you!" I hugged her so hard she squeaked, then begged her to go downstairs and distract him while I dressed. I was a whirlwind. Five minutes later, teeth brushed, face washed, jeaned and T-shirted, I ran downstairs. There he was, chatting easily on the couch with my starstruck little sister. He stood when I walked in. Portia looked from me to him and back to me again.

"Want to go for a ride?" he asked.

"Can I come?" Portia piped up.

"Another time," I promised, never taking my eyes from his.

We drove back to our spot on the Harpeth River and sat on some boulders on the riverbank. He'd told Sara the truth, that he wanted to be an actor and didn't want to live a certain way just because it was expected of him. She said he was being ridiculous and he'd break his mother's heart.

One other thing. She claimed it was all my fault.

When he finished, we just sat there, watching the muddy river flow. He took my hand. He kissed me. I laid my cheek on his chest, listening to the steady beating of his heart. And nothing else mattered. Nothing else mattered at all.

9

The teen information superhighway being what it is, no formal announcement was necessary. As I headed from the parking lot to the high school on Monday morning, I was dissected under a social microscope, components examined and categorized, compared and contrasted.

Sara's hair is better. Kate's breasts are larger.

Sara's butt is perfect. Kate's legs are longer.

Most of all: Sara is one of us. Kate isn't.

Jack and Sara were Redford royalty, and an invading Yankee infidel had toppled the queen from her throne. That it had been Jack's choice was irrelevant. In the eyes of Sara and her minions, I was solely to blame. They demanded vengeance.

By the end of the school day, someone had scrawled BITCH on my locker. On Tuesday, I found dog crap on the hood of my car. Jack couldn't believe his ex or any of her friends had done these things. I had suspicions but no proof. Fortunately, by Wednesday, the hubbub died down, hopefully forever.

We spent all our time together. Where you found Jack, you found Kate. The warm September days melted into each other like cherry Popsicles, leaving the same sweetness behind. Only the occasional breath of autumn on a breeze promised the coming change of seasons. Sometimes on weekends, Jack and I would hike in the hills outside of town to a distant sulfur spring that he said was first tapped by his great-great-grandfather. At night, we'd sit on a blanket near the river, his arms wrapped around me, sharing anything and everything, all that little stuff that seems so unimportant until you're in love. How I once threw up in front of my whole second-grade class, and how I had never wanted to face those kids again. How the tiny scar on his left thumb was from a fishhook—he and Chaz had ditched school and gone fishing, but they'd gotten caught because they couldn't get the hook out of Jack's thumb. His mom had made him apologize not only to his teacher, but also to the principal and to the chief of police.

The more I got to know Jack, the more I realized that, in the sense of being a good human being, he was probably the best person I had ever known. He did a lot of volunteer work, but was very low-key about it. For example, he was a volunteer aide at Warren Elementary's afterschool program. Warren was Redford's poorest and lowest-achieving grade school. Jack tutored the kids and he coached their soccer team, the Strikers. He came up with jobs for them so they could earn spending money. He invented awards like Most Improved or Best Team Player. The awards came with gift certificates to clothing stores, bookstores, and the Redford Cinema. Needless to say, the Strikers adored him.

The smallest, toughest kid on the team was Cooper Wilson, a scrawny eight-year-old with carrot-orange hair and the bopping gait of a born athlete. He lived in a doublewide mobile home with his older sister and his mom. They were on food stamps. Jack told me that when he had first met Cooper, it had been in the vice principal's office, after Cooper had beaten up a kid who'd called him white trash. Evidently, he got called white trash on a pretty regular basis.

Then there was Cooper, post-Jack. Jack tutored him, shot hoops with him, and, under the guise of hanging out, dropped by Cooper's house with groceries. Cooper started using the word "Jack" in most of his sentences and quit getting into fights. He'd come to Strikers practice half an hour early and just sit there waiting for Jack to arrive. And when he did, Cooper's face was the sun.

Jack also worked at Peace Inn, a temporary shelter for troubled teenagers. Kids would ring the buzzer at all hours;

a volunteer was always available to help them through the night. Sometimes that person was Jack. He inspired me so much that I started doing volunteer work with him. It made me feel good about myself. Besides, it was the best way to spend a lot of time with him.

Other than passion for each other, the greatest love we shared was for the stage. Sometimes we'd go to the theater in Nashville and afterward stay late at the Peace Inn, discussing the play over endless cups of coffee. I showed him my work; we read scenes aloud. We laughed and talked and shared our dreams. And we kissed until we were breathless.

My New York friends weighed in by phone. Nia said she didn't care how much volunteer work the boy did or how well he knew Chekhov, falling for a guy whose mother was past president of the local chapter of the United Daughters of the Confederacy was lunacy. BB counseled me to check for eyeholes in the sheets on Jack's bed. Only Lillith suggested that I go for it, reasoning that my relationship with Jack was so hot that it would undoubtedly go down in flames, but meanwhile I should enjoy the inferno.

Before Jack, the hip, arch, jaded me would have said the same things. I'd decided long ago that all those romantic movies where girl gets guy and lives happily ever after were fairy tales. Half of my friends had parents whose marriages had cracked up. The ones that were still intact didn't seem all that terrific. It's not like I ever saw longing in my mother's eyes when she looked at my father.

So maybe I had fantasized about a guy who'd be smart and strong, and passionate and gentle, too. A guy so giving he'd spend time with a lonely kid before he'd hang out with his friends. A guy I could be entirely myself with, who cared about the things I cared about, who *knew* me, and who I knew in return. But I never really believed that such a guy existed. Until Jack Redford transcended my disillusioned dreams.

10

I was breathless on the Wednesday evening in late September when I sprinted from my house to the Pink Teacup. I knew I was already ten minutes late to meet Mrs. Augustus—pretty rude considering that I'd been the one to ask for the meeting. Through the front glass, I saw her seated at a small, round table for two, its glass top anchoring a teacup-patterned, lacy pink tablecloth. Standing near her, holding a white bakery bag tied with a pink ribbon, was Mr. Derry. He ran the local Shell station. He'd fixed a flat on my car the week before and had refused to charge me, though he did lecture me about keeping my tires properly inflated.

"I'm so sorry to be late," I apologized as I hurried toward Mrs. Augustus.

"It's fine, dear. You gave me a chance to catch up with Mr. Derry."

He hoisted the paper bag. I could see a translucent butter spot blossoming on the bottom. "Good visiting with you, " Mr. Derry told Mrs. Augustus. Then he turned to Birdie, who was behind the counter, patiently helping a young girl and her mother pick out a treat from the glass display case. "And thank you, Birdie. You know the missus has been having one of her cravings."

"Now, Judson Derry, where are your manners?" Birdie mock scolded. "Can't you see I'm helping Shanika here choose a very important cookie?"

"Momma says the tooth fairy wants me to get my favorite," the little girl told Birdie as her mother beamed down at her.

"Well, tooth fairies do that kind of thing," Birdie told her. "So you take your time, honey." She raised her voice and called to Mr. Derry again. "You just remember, Judson, a pregnant woman in her ninth month who doesn't satisfy her food cravings gives birth to a sickly baby. And I know you want Judson Junior to be fat and sassy like his daddy."

Mr. Derry laughed. "Hey, now."

"You tell Lurlene I'll come by and see her this weekend," Birdie promised as the little girl pointed to a butterscotch chocolate chip cookie the size of a small Frisbee. Birdie snared it for her with a piece of pink tissue paper.

"Good choice there, Shanika!" Mr. Derry exclaimed, then turned back to Mrs. Augustus and me. "Mrs. Augustus, don't you go driving that car all the way to Tuscaloosa again before I do an oil change, hear? You're due."

"I'll ask my husband to bring it in, thank you, Mr. Derry."

"My pleasure, ma'am. You know the Mapco won't give you any kind of service." He fixed his eyes on me. "You keeping them tires filled, young lady?"

"Uh . . . I'll have to check."

He shook his head as if I'd disappointed him. "You get your daddy to buy you a pressure gauge."

"Yes, sir," I found myself saying.

The answer seemed to satisfy him. He said some more good-byes, tarried at the front door to greet another of his customers, and finally left. When he was gone, I sat opposite Mrs. Augustus and tried to explain why I was late. "My sister was having a crisis over some horrid girl in her class named Madison."

"Madison Honeywell?"

"I only know her as Madison the Cool. Or Madison the Cruel, depending on whether or not she's nice to my sister that day."

"Well, if it's Madison Honeywell at Redford East Middle School, her uncle Frank is my sister's nephew."

I felt the heat rush to my face. "I'm sorry. I'm sure Madison is a nice girl—"

Mrs. Augustus waved away the rest of my statement.

"Nonsense. Madison Honeywell is as unpleasant as a wet possum."

I smiled. "I thought Southerners didn't say mean things about each other."

"Go on! We're just creative about it." She chuckled. "Here's an example. Every new mother thinks her new child is a beauty. But sometimes a new baby is just bald, drooling, and ugly. Well, of course, no one is going to tell a new mother that her child is pitiful looking. A Yankee might lie to spare the mother's feelings: 'Oh, your baby is just so cute.' But a Southerner'll look at the child and say, 'Now *there's* a baby!'"

I laughed.

"And the mother says thank you and feels you've paid her a lovely compliment," Mrs. Augustus concluded. "And that, my dear, is very, *very* Southern. So, shall we have some of Birdie's fruit tea while we chat?"

As we waited for Birdie to bring the icy tea, I got my cassette recorder ready. "Everyone says if I want to really know Redford's racial history, I should speak with you."

"Yes, I'm a living fossil," she teased. "So this play you're planning to write will be about Redford?"

"I think so. I'm not really sure yet." I fiddled with the microphone. "Do you mind if I tape you?"

"Not at all."

"Two glasses of my best fruit tea," Birdie sang out, setting the frosted pink glasses on the table. "And something to nibble on." She plunked a pink platter of fragrant cookies, fat with chocolate chips, in the center of the table. "Straight out of the oven. You know you can't drink my tea without my cookies, Mrs. Augustus."

"Indeed I do, Birdie, dear." Mrs. Augustus reached for one. "Have you tried these yet, Kate? They're heavenly."

"Oh, sure she has," Birdie put in. "Me and Kate are buddies already. I met her on her first day in Redford. Well, I'll let you two visit. Don't let me catch you leavin' any crumbs." She grinned over her shoulder as she departed.

"She's really nice." I bit into a warm cookie and felt a chocolate chip melt onto my tongue.

"Birdie's grandmother opened the Pink Teacup in 1928," Mrs. Augustus told me, then took a contemplative sip of tea. "Her name was Florence, but everyone called her Florrie. She was my mother's dearest friend."

I nodded and switched on my recorder.

"My mother brought me here on opening day," she went on. "I believe I was eight years old at the time. Miss Florrie was an unmarried woman, and she'd hired a black man as her baker. Mr. Samuel Brewster, his name was. He taught Miss Florrie how to make those cookies you're eating. Everyone thought they were keeping company. It was quite a scandal."

"How do you remember all this?" I marveled.

"Memory's a funny thing." Mrs. Augustus patted her lips with the pale pink linen napkin. "Half the time I can't remember where I put my glasses, but I remember things from seventy years ago as if they happened yesterday.

Anyway, Mr. Brewster's grandfather was a slave who had been freed by Birdie's great-great-grandfather a year before the Battle of Redford, which was in November of 1863."

"What made him do that?"

"I heard he was a very religious man. I believe he prayed on it and simply came to the conclusion that one human being owning another human being went against the Bible."

"How could anyone come to any *other* conclusion?"

"You must understand, Kate. It was a very different time then—a different world, really. It took a hundred years after that war for real change to come." She paused for another sip of tea. "When I was your parents' age, there were signs posted everywhere: Whites Only. Colored Drinking Fountain. Blacks couldn't stay at most hotels or eat at most restaurants. There were laws about it. Jim Crow laws, they were called, after a Negro minstrel—it was a terrible and insulting name. Essentially, they were a way to make blacks second-class citizens. And not just in the South, either, my dear."

I rested my chin on my cupped hand. "It just seems so . . . so . . . ."

"Ugly," she filled in. "I have a cousin in Danville, Virginia. Bernice Abernathy. She's a librarian, too. I recall—I believe it was around 1960 when the segregation laws were repealed—her library took all the tables and chairs out of the library rather than have blacks sit with whites. You had to pick up your books and just carry them on out."

"What about here, Mrs. Augustus? Did your library do that?"

"No, my dear. I'm pleased to say we did not. But we had our own problems." Mrs. Augustus reached for another cookie. "You know Jimmy Mack's restaurant?"

"Sure. Right across the square."

"It was whites only till 1961."

I couldn't believe it. "You're kidding."

"No, my dear, I most certainly am not. Do you know about the sit-ins?"

I tried to recall what I'd read somewhere. "Where . . . blacks went into restaurants and tried to get served?"

She nodded. "In 1961, there were big ones in Nashville at the Woolworth's lunch counter. Not long after that, Lucas Roberts integrated Jimmy Mack's."

I was surprised Nikki hadn't mentioned this to me. "You mean Reverend Roberts? Nikki's father? She's a friend of mine."

"Well, then you have excellent taste in friends. Back in those days, Lucas Roberts was a student at Fisk. He and nine other students walked right through the front door of Jimmy Mack's. The boys wore jackets and ties. The girls wore lovely dresses. They took seats at two tables and waited. All the white people were served. But these ten young people were ignored. So they sat there all day, in silence."

I stopped her, checked my tape to be sure it was recording properly, and then restarted it. "Go on, please," I urged her. "What happened?"

"Well, when Jimmy Mack III closed at the end of the day, these young students came outside to find white folks lined up on the sidewalk cursing them and waving the Confederate battle flag."

My hand flew to my mouth. "That's disgusting."

"Yes. It is. But in the long run, the black students won."

I dreaded asking the question I was about to pose because I liked her so much. But I had to ask anyway. "Mrs. Augustus, were you there that day?"

"Yes, I was."

"What did you do?"

"It's right that you should ask me that." She sipped the last of her tea until the straw gurgled in the chips of ice. "Those white folks—they were my friends and neighbors. I tried to get them to stop. So did Birdie's mother. But they wouldn't listen."

"The two of you tried, Mrs. Augustus. That's the important thing."

She shook her head. "The truth is, until that sit-in, I hadn't done anything. I lived in a world where my black neighbors were used and abused, and I didn't see it because I did not want to see it. I shall feel ashamed of that for the rest of my life."

She stirred her ice with her straw, and I could see that her thoughts were far away. "I know this will be difficult for you to understand, Kate. I still love that flag. I used to fly that flag from my front porch with great pride. It was the banner of the soldiers, not the Confederacy. My grandfather died in battle under that flag; so did Birdie's ancestor—the one who freed his own slave. But after that day at Jimmy Mack's, I brought it inside. I haven't flown it since."

I mused on that for a moment. "Jack says you're the smartest person he knows. Now I know why."

She smiled. "Well, I'm certain he's wrong, but it was a very kind thing for him to say. He's a special boy, you know."

I nodded. Words couldn't begin to explain everything I felt for Jack.

She leaned forward. "Yes. I see in your eyes that you know how special he is. His family owned many slaves. You know that."

I nodded again.

"The sins of the father are not visited upon the son, my dear. But Jack's people come from that world; they're still a part of it, in a certain way."

"He's not, though," I protested.

"Yes, Kate. He is." She wrapped her elegant fingers around her glass and looked into the melting ice slivers as if she were reading tea leaves. "It's much more complicated than you think. Or than he thinks, I expect. My advice—not that you should take love advice from an old lady—is to go slowly. Fools rush in, my dear. Only fools rush in."

In my head the words formed: It's already too late for that. Much too late.

11

*For all the time Jack and I spent to*gether, we didn't spend much of it with his friends. I told myself I liked it better that way, that we didn't need anyone else. But on a Saturday in early October when he finally asked me to join him and his buds at Jimmy Mack's, I was more than happy. To me it represented a kind of acceptance and belonging that could only bring Jack and me even closer. However skeptical his friends were about his relationship with me, I was sure I could win them over.

Before we went to Jimmy Mack's, though, there was a Strikers game on the battered schoolyard at Warren Elementary. I stood on the sidelines and cheered as they took on the Cougars from Johnson Elementary. Most of the game was a scoreless tie. Then, with thirty seconds to go, Cooper Wilson booted home the winning goal. The Strikers went wild. I think I screamed louder than anyone.

We took the team out for pizza afterward, then waited for some straggler parents to pick up their kids. When Cooper's mom didn't show—which happened fairly often—we drove him home. Jack had bestowed on him the Most Committed Player award, which came with a gift certificate to the local bookstore, and Cooper was so excited that he practically vibrated out of his seat belt. He ran into his mobile home, bursting to tell someone about it. His sister, dressed for work at Hooters, was making out with her boyfriend in the living room. She barely looked up as Cooper tried to tell her about the game and the award. Finally, his mom pulled up in her bomber of a car, full of apologies. Only then did we depart.

Jack had already introduced me to a few of Redford's traditions, like Friday home football games under the lights. On the way to Jimmy Mack's, he introduced me to another one, "Flipping the Dip." Teens in Redford made fun of Flipping the Dip, but they still did it—driving the length of Main Street, circling the monument, and then doing a U-turn at Mr. Derry's Shell station. Jack said that scores of Redford romances had been kindled while Flipping the Dip, and we did a two-lap homage before heading to Jimmy Mack's to meet up with his friends.

Jimmy Mack's was another Redford tradition. The football team ate there every Friday before home games—joined by half the town—in a ritual called Puttin' on the Feed: fried chicken, sides, biscuits, gravy, all the sweet tea you could drink. Of course, as Mrs. Augustus had explained to me, in the not-so-good old days, you could only partake if you were white. Now, allegedly, people of every race, creed, and stripe were welcome. But just as kids at Redford High self-segregated in the bleachers and the cafeteria, black kids almost never set foot in Jimmy Mack's. They hung out around the corner at Taco Bell.

The entryway to Jimmy Mack's is adorned with photos of Redford High's football team, dating back to World War II. Behind the cash register, there's an array of flags: American, Tennessee . . . and Confederate. So you can imagine how odd it seemed when we were hit with a wall of hip-hop music as soon as we walked in. A group of black kids spilled out of a back booth, music blasting from a portable CD player.

From the other direction: "Yo, Redford!"

It was Chaz, waving to us from a table near the front window. He had one beefy arm slung casually around the shoulders of his girlfriend, Crystal Chambers. Crystal was Sara's best friend, and I realized that she was the one who'd been with Sara during the sorority hazing I'd witnessed on the football field my first day at Redford High. With Chaz and Crystal were Terry Collins and Tisha White, two other seniors. Tisha was in my American history class. I liked her. I was relieved to see that Sara wasn't part of the group.

Jack and I squeezed into a couple of empty seats as a new groove erupted from the boom box. Crystal covered her ears. "That music is driving me nuts!"

Chaz shrugged. "I already complained to the waitress, baby."

"Well, complain to someone else, then."

"Where's Big Jimmy?" Jack asked. Big Jimmy was Jimmy Mack IV, who owned the place.

"Sliced a finger on the meat cutter, went for stitches," Crystal told Jack. Evidently eye contact with me would have been disloyal to Sara, so she rendered me invisible. But Tisha noticed and came to my rescue.

"Cute shirt, Kate," she said supportively.

I smiled, grateful that she was being nice. "Thanks."

A harried, elderly waitress with dishes balanced on her arms stepped up to our booth. "Blue-cheese burger?"

"Right here, ma'am," Chaz said as loud laughter erupted from the rear booth. A tall guy I didn't recognize was standing in the aisle, rapping along to the music. "Ma'am, if there's no one here can handle those people back there, I'm fixing to do it myself."

"Knock yourself out, cowboy." She distributed the rest of the food, took Jack's and my orders, and hustled off to the kitchen.

"You and what army?" Jack teased.

Chaz pointed at him. "If push comes to shove, I know you got my back, Redford."

Jack nodded. "Always."

Thankfully, the music dropped a few decibels. Crystal pushed back a lock of dark hair and finally glanced in my direction. "So, Kate. How's it going?"

"Okay."

"I'm sure it's hard to be new and not fit in," she said sweetly, stirring a pool of catsup with a French fry.

"Meow," Tisha whined at Crystal's dis.

"What?" Crystal asked. As if she didn't know.

"I think she's fitting in just fine," Jack said.

The conversation turned to football, Redford's unofficial religion. Chaz had just been named starting tight end. Everyone was excited this year about the Rebels' chances of winning the league championship. It hadn't happened in a decade.

Crystal giggled. "Remember last year, Jackson, after the South Columbia game? We got wasted, and Sara dared us to go skinny dipping in the river?"

"'Bout froze my ass off!" Chaz hooted. Everyone laughed. Anxiety fizzed up in me like an Alka-Seltzer. Jack was a part of them in a way I never could be.

The waitress came back to the table with our Cokes. The football discussion continued, and I continued to have nothing much to say until an odd-looking man entered the restaurant. Rail thin with a long beard, he wore ancient gray woolen trousers with a long jacket and cap and carried a canteen, a shoulder bag, and a vintage rifle.

"What's up with that?" I asked, nudging my chin in his direction.

"Bo Alford, curator of the Battle of Redford Museum," Terry said, sipping his Coke. "On Saturday afternoons, he plays dress-up and leads tours. The beard's fake, but all the clothes are a hundred and forty years old. So's the gun."

I made a mental note to try to interview Mr. Alford for my play. Not that this play actually existed. The week before, I'd talked to Nikki's father, as well as Malik El Baz, a black activist lawyer in Nashville. Reverend Lucas had been thoughtful; El Baz, fiery. I'd been trying to get an interview with a local white separatist leader named Ron Bingham who'd been profiled in the *Tennessean*. He lived forty miles south of Redford in the small town of Pulaski. But though I'd sent e-mails and left phone messages, the closest I'd come to actual contact was when his wife hung up on me.

After each new interview I'd sit down at my computer, hands poised over the keyboard, waiting for inspiration to strike. Evidently, inspiration was busy striking some other lucky writer, because everything I wrote seemed worse than the previous effort. I'd end up deleting it all, sending it—with all the other attempts—to the cosmic trash bin where really bad writing goes.

Tisha rolled her eyes. "That reenactment stuff is *so* hokey."

Terry nudged her playfully. "Hey, where's your Southern pride, girl?"

"Up my ass," Tisha deadpanned.

I laughed. The problem was, no one laughed with me.

Though Jack gave my hand a reassuring squeeze, my cheeks burned.

"Hey, I'm with Kate," Tisha said. "You can't take that crap seriously."

Chaz wagged a finger at her. "You don't mess with tradition."

"That is such a load of bull," Tisha insisted. "The thing is—"

We lost the rest of Tisha's sentence as the hip-hop was cranked back up to earsplitting volume.

"That's it." Chaz half stood and twisted around, cupping his hands around his mouth. "Hey, could y'all turn it down a little?"

One of the black kids leaned into the aisle. It was Nikki's brother, Luke.

"Yo, I said, turn it down!" Chaz repeated.

Instantly, Luke and another guy were sauntering toward us, coiled rage beneath ebony skin. "You talking to me?" Luke asked when they got within spitting distance.

Chaz stood to meet his challenge. "I'm just asking for y'all to turn down your music, bro."

Luke edged closer. "Do I look like your bro?"

Chaz held his palms up. "Look, I'm not trying to start anything. But if you start it, I'll finish it."

"Why don't you get your cracker buddy to lend you one of his sheets, *bro.*" Luke jutted his chin toward Mr. Alford.

"Jeez, man, you got a chip on your shoul—"

The front door swung open. A huge man who had to be Big Jimmy followed his massive stomach into the restaurant. "What in the Sam Hill is goin' on?" he bellowed, gesturing toward the offending CD player. With a heavily bandaged middle finger, he looked as if he was flipping everyone the bird.

"I already asked them to turn it down, Big Jimmy," Chaz said.

Big Jimmy waddled toward Luke. "I *said*, turn that crap off!" he thundered.

Luke nodded toward his friends. The hip-hop went silent.

"You people are welcome in my establishment just like anyone else," Big Jimmy told Luke. "But you play my jukebox or you play nothing."

Luke feigned incomprehension and cupped his ear. "Could you repeat that, suh? Cuz you knows we people is kinda slow."

Big Jimmy glowered. "Don't give me that bull, Luke Roberts. Do I need to call your daddy?"

I couldn't imagine Luke Roberts backing off because someone threatened to call his daddy. But to my surprise, after a brief staredown, he turned away, pulling his friends in his wake. They threw some money at the cash register and dodged around a skinny white couple in matching NASCAR T-shirts. The male half of the couple did an exaggerated double take as Luke and his friends stormed out the door.

Crystal groaned. "Oh no. It's Boozer and the Skank."

"Heading this way," Tisha added.

Now I recognized them from the under-the-bleachers, nicotine-for-lunch bunch. They were indeed heading right for us. "Who are they?"

"Jared Boose and his girlfriend, Sandy Kincaid," Tisha said.

"Better known as the Skank," Crystal added. "Low on the food chain. She actually tried to join Crimson Maidens her freshman year. It was so pathetic."

Sandy Kincaid didn't look like someone I'd have any particular desire to know either. But something about Crystal's comment rubbed against the grain. "I thought Crimson Maidens was open to anyone," I said, all innocence, curious to see how she'd respond.

"Oh, sorry, Kate, but you needed to sign up the first week of school," Crystal replied. "I don't think you'd enjoy it all that much anyway. It's just a bunch of girls who—"

"Hey, 'sup, Slick?" Jared asked, offering Jack the latest variation of a fist bump. Jack was too polite not to do it with him. Crystal didn't get to finish her sentence, and I didn't get a chance to explain that I knew all I needed to know about Crimson Maidens. Like I would ever want to be a part of *that* little club.

"What the hell was Luke and them gorillas doing in here?" Jared went on. "Taco Bell ain't good enough all of a sudden?"

"I guess they didn't want tacos," Jack said, his voice even.

Jared smirked. "Yeah, they wanted 'em some *white* meat."

"*So* not funny," Tisha snapped.

"Don't get your panties in a wad, girl. Hey, was Nikki and them out front when y'all got here? They're still harassin' people to sign their damn petition."

Jared's unvarnished racism and the oh-so-superior attitude of Jack's friends was making me insane. "You mean this petition?" I plucked a copy out of my purse. The temperature dropped enough to flash-freeze the burgers, but I plunged on. "Anyone care to sign?"

Jared jeered at Jack. "You better get your lady in line, Slick."

Through clenched teeth, Jack told Jared to stop calling him Slick. And to mind his own business. And to get his own table. Now. Jared looked like he wanted to lob a comeback but didn't have the nerve. So he and Sandy slunk off.

"Thank you, Lord," Tisha said.

"Kate?" Chaz pointed to my petition, which was still on our table, one corner now soaked in iced tea. "Could you put that thing back where it came from?"

"What do you have against a vote?" I asked. "This is America, that's how we decide things."

Chaz shook his head. "Having a vote would just be just the tip of the iceberg. What comes next? See, what these people really want is to take away our heritage. You're not from here, there's no way you can understand."

I plucked the petition from the wet spot. "I'm trying to understand. To me, that flag just stands for racism."

"Lord, I'm sick of hearing that," Crystal declared. "I love that flag, and I don't have a racist bone in my body."

"That's what I'm saying," Chaz agreed. He clapped Jack on the back. "Tell her how it be, Redford."

"I think Kate has a point," Jack said.

Chaz chuckled. "What, I'm a racist now?"

"I'm just saying that if some students are offended, why not let everyone vote on it?" Jack asked.

"I don't have a problem with that," Terry said, backing Jack up.

"Well, Terry, I'm sure some students are offended by the American flag," Crystal drawled sarcastically. "Maybe we'd better take a vote on that, too."

Chaz elbowed Jack playfully. "Just remember, guy: The Pride of Southern manhood rests on your last-o'-the-Redford-line shoulders."

"How about if my mom adopts you, so the pride can rest on *your* shoulders?" Jack snapped.

"Get out of town, Redford," Chaz guffawed. "Next thing you're gonna say you've signed that thing."

"No," he said. "I haven't."

"Yet." It popped out of my mouth before I could stop myself. Some crazed part of me needed to make my stand, here and now. I looked over at Jack. "McSorley's deadline is Monday. Last I heard, we're still about twenty signatures short."

Chaz's eyebrows headed for his hairline. "You seriously think my boy would sign for you?"

"No," I said. "I think he'll sign because it's the right thing to do."

"And *I* think you don't know what the hell you're talking about," Chaz said, glowering.

"Let's just drop it," Jack suggested.

But I wouldn't. I couldn't. Not with his best friend sneering at me like that. "Maybe you didn't get the memo, Chaz," I told him. "The war is over. Your side lost. Deal with it."

His cold eyes held mine. "Jackson Redford ain't turning on his own. I don't care how hot your little tail is."

Jack yanked Chaz to his feet. "Don't you ever talk to her like that."

"Why, the truth hurt?" Chaz taunted.

Terry banged his hands on the table so hard the cutlery jumped. "Dammit, will y'all just chill? You're both acting like jackasses."

Jack let go of Chaz. Then he grabbed the petition and scrawled his name. At the same moment, Nikki swung through the front door.

"Hey, Nikki!" I heard Jared shout at her. "Bring your petition over here, girl. I'll sign. With this!" He made an obscene gesture toward his crotch, and Nikki pivoted away from him toward the ladies' room. But she had to duck around Big Jimmy, who was coming on the run from the kitchen, smacking the flat end of a meat cleaver against his uninjured hand.

"Dammit, Jared Boose! That kinda talk ain't welcome in my establishment!"

"Aw, I'm just funnin', Big Jimmy," Jared said. Then he caught Chaz's eye and flashed him a cocky thumbs-up.

Disgusted, Jack pushed back from the table. "Let's get out of here," he told me.

"Come on, Jack," Chaz protested. "I'm nothing like that low-life cretin Boose. You know that." He offered Jack his hand—a clear peace offering.

Jack hesitated, then shook with Chaz. "Yeah, man. I know."

"We're cool?" Chaz asked him.

"Yeah."

Chaz grinned and smacked his left hand on top of their handshake. "You can't cut me loose that easy, Redford. And I always got your back, man. Always."

12

I continued to be nice to Jack's friends, but except for Terry and Tisha, they continued to be cold to me. The fact that I'd helped Nikki get enough signatures for a vote on the flag—and that Jack's was one of those signatures—certainly didn't bring us any closer. Somehow, they forgave him and blamed me.

The night Nikki turned in our signatures there was a big celebration at her church. My whole family came, but Jack didn't. I told myself it was okay. After all, he'd signed the petition in front of his friends. He mentored kids of all different colors who needed help. He was totally supportive of *Black and White and Redford All Over;* he'd even said he'd make some calls and try to get me an interview with the Klan guy. So what more could I possibly want from him?

A voice inside my head answered: You want him to stand with you. Not just in front of his friends, but in front of everyone. You want him to choose.

The next day, McSorley announced that the signatures were certified. After that, we waited all week for him to say when the vote on the new team name and emblem would take place. Friday morning, a memo was posted outside his office. The vote would be in four weeks, right after midterms. Some of Nikki's friends claimed that McSorley was buying time until he could think of a way to get out of the vote. And some of Jack's friends hoped that was exactly what would happen.

Jack and I came to an understanding. He'd hang out with his friends when I was with Nikki or when I was doing interviews for my alleged play (alleged in that I *still* hadn't actually written anything) or transcribing my notes. Then he'd come over and listen to the tapes with me. My family was always happy to see him. Jack was a parent's dream: polite, smart, handsome, rich, same name as the town. That kind of thing.

School was more complicated. Jack's friends were omnipresent, and so was the tension. Also, Miss Bright was furious with both of us. Jack hadn't auditioned for *Living in Sunshine.* Instead, we'd told her—even though she claimed she'd written the lead role especially with him in mind—that we both just wanted to be on the set construction crew. Somehow, that was my fault, too.

In a late-night phone call, Lillith tried to put the whole thing in perspective. "Okay, it's not like they're Nazis," she said. "Nazis are scary. These people are just pathetic, stuck in some weird Civil War time warp. You can't blame Jack. He's just like this guy I know who has six toes. I mean, he was born that way."

Typical Lillith logic. I really missed her. I told her how Jack had invited me for dinner the next night because he wanted me to meet his mother, and how his mother, Sally Redford, was to Redford what the queen of England was to . . . well, you get the picture. And one other thing. Jack's house didn't have a street address, because it didn't need one. Everyone just knew it as Redford House.

• • •

I stared at my reflection in the mirror above my dresser: Stretchy shirt that ended an inch above the top of low-cut jeans. Leather jacket. Primped and painted just enough to make it look as if I hadn't, I hoped. I was nervous. I told myself it was only dinner at my boyfriend's house, no big deal, but the Hell's Angels popping wheelies in my stomach weren't listening.

Portia sat on the window seat under the eaves, living vicariously through my preparations. "Why would you wear that to dinner?"

"Because my studded dog collar is in the laundry." I rummaged for earrings in my jewelry box.

"I told you, Kate. Cool girls here don't wear jeans and belly shirts. And they definitely don't wear them to dinner at Redford House." She came to stand by me, twisting to check out the rear view of her new boot-cut black pants. "Does my butt look big in these?"

"No."

She sprayed herself with my perfume and sniffed the air. "Dee-lish. Can I wear some next Friday night?"

I reached for my hairbrush. "What's next Friday night?"

"The home game against Franklin West, silly. I'm going with Cassidy." Cassidy was her new thank-God-she-had-one best friend. "Hey, guess what? This boy likes me. His name is Barney. I know he has a dumb name, but he's nice. He read *Childhood's End* even before I did. He and this other guy Alan are going to the game, too. What should I wear so I don't look fat?"

We saw our mother in the mirror at the same time she appeared in the doorway. "You aren't fat, Portia."

Portia folded her arms. "You weren't supposed to hear."

"I gathered." My mom took in my outfit and frowned. "You're wearing *that* to Redford House?"

"Thank you!" Portia sang out.

I groaned. "Will everyone please give it a rest? It's *just a place where people live.*"

"So is Buckingham Palace," Portia remarked.

"Portia, there's no need to make your sister nervous," my mom said. "She's perfectly capable of handling herself in any situation." She turned to me. "Oh, by the way, Kate. Your father picked up some flowers for you to take with you."

"He did? Since when does Dad remember flowers?"

My mother laughed. "Since his daughter got invited to dinner at Redford House."

• • •

Redford House was like Tara, only bigger. And behind locked gates.

With a tasteful bouquet nestled on the seat next to me, I turned my Saturn onto Redford House's private road. Jack's directions had been: Follow the road to the electric gate and announce yourself over the intercom. When the gate opens, stay on the twisty driveway up to the house.

As it turned out, I didn't have to. Because Jack was leaning against the open gate, waiting for me. I exhaled the breath I hadn't realized I'd been holding. He stuck out a thumb. "Hitch a lift, lady?"

"Depends. What are your intentions?"

"Bad."

"Good. Get in."

It was so much easier to enter the double front doors holding his hand. We had just stepped into a majestic foyer when Jack's mother seemed to float in from nowhere. Sally Redford was pretty, in a beige dress that fell just below the knee, real pearls, and chin-length hair sprayed into submission. Though I knew she was about the same age as my mom, she seemed older. My mother didn't own a tasteful beige below-the-knee dress. Or hair spray. And Jensen Pride would sooner get a navel ring than wear pearls. Apparently, the only thing our mothers had in common was childbirth.

Mrs. Redford took my hand in hers. "You must be Kate."

"I must be." My cheeks burned as I instantly realized how snotty that must have sounded; I hadn't meant to be. Was my hand sweating? I thrust the flowers at her and surreptitiously wiped my palms on my jeans.

"Flowers. Lovely." She smiled Jack's smile and spoke with the same soft drawl. "Jackson has talked so much about you, Kate."

She went to get a vase, and Jack led me into a formal living room. The furniture was mahogany, substantial-looking, and very old. Probably worth a mint. Not a Barcalounger in sight. I noticed a cigarette burn on a side table and a long, coppery stain on one of the tapestry carpets.

Jack excused himself to go help his mother. I looked around. One wall was covered with locked display cases. Some held daggers, muskets, or rifles; others contained uniforms and medals. The opposite wall featured oil paintings of men in uniform. I drifted over to read the brass plaques beneath the ornate frames. They were portraits of Jack's ancestors. The oldest one was General Eustis Redford of the Continental Army. Born London, England, 1731; died Yorktown, Virginia, 1781. Next to him was Major General Jackson Redford. Born Charleston, South Carolina, 1819; United States Army, 1839–1849, Army of Tennessee (Redford's Division, Cheatham's Corps) 1861–1863; died Battle of Redford, Redford, Tennessee, 1863.

I shuddered. If I fast-forwarded Jack twenty-five years and gave him a long beard, he'd be a dead ringer for Major General Redford.

Mrs. Redford returned with the flowers in a crystal vase. Jack followed with a tray of cheese and crackers and a pitcher of fruit tea. "That's our wall of service," Mrs. Redford said as she placed the vase on a side table.

"A lot of soldiers." I winced inwardly at my vapid comment. Gee, Kate, I guess that's why she called it a *wall of service.*

She smiled fondly at her son. "Our family has a proud military tradition. Jack's father was a fighter pilot. He was lost on a mission ten years ago."

"I'm so sorry," I said. I'd wondered how Jack's father had died but hadn't wanted to bring it up.

"Mom," Jack protested, running a hand through his hair. "I haven't even had a chance to tell Kate about that yet."

"It's nothing to hide, Jackson. I know you're as proud of your father as I am." She turned to me. "My son is the last of the Redford men. Until he has a son of his own one day."

What could I possibly say to that? I almost offered to jump Jack on the dining room table so she'd have a Redford heir.

"My family's story is kind of Shakespearean," Jack said, his voice tight.

"Please, sit." Mrs. Redford gestured for me to have a seat on the couch. Jack joined me. His mother chose a wing chair. "I noticed you looking at the rug before, Kate," she said, indicating the rust-colored oblong stain. "That's where General Redford's men laid him after he was wounded. They carried him home from the field of battle; he died right there."

No flipping way. That was a *bloodstain*? Who *keeps* a rug like that?

We sipped fruit tea and she asked the usual questions about my family. Though she smiled throughout my answers, I could tell she was less than impressed with my parents' degrees from Rutgers University and my New Jersey roots.

"So, Kate, did your father serve?" she asked.

"Yes, he did," I assured her.

"Oh really?" She eagerly awaited my elaboration.

"Absolutely. He was a waiter in college." I meant this as a joke—that seemed pretty obvious to me—but no one laughed. "Kidding," I added lamely.

Mrs. Redford smiled thinly, as if I'd just farted but she was too well-bred to point it out. Then she suggested that it might be a good time for us to eat dinner. She led us to a formal dining room, where the table was lavishly set, with a floral centerpiece that put my offering to shame.

"We don't eat in here every night," Jack said, winking at me. "Just when we want to impress someone special."

In the dining room, too, the walls were adorned with history: the Redford family tree, the Tennessee state constitution, and the charter for the town of Redford. "The constitution and charter are original documents," Mrs. Redford said as Jack pulled out her chair, then mine. "We're very fortunate to have them."

A gray-haired African American woman in a starched uniform brought out serving dishes from the kitchen. Wilted spinach salad was followed by leg of lamb. Jack was funny and sweet, smoothing over any rough spots, doing his best to buff me into his mother's good graces. He got her to talk about her volunteer work, a subject she loved. From how she described it, it was more than a full-time job. In addition to being chair of the Redford Historical Preservation Society and on the boards of various Nashville charities, she did many hands-on things, like helping the teenagers maintain vegetable and flower gardens behind the Peace Inn. She was also one of the founders of Redford Women United, whose mission was to help single mothers get off welfare. There, Mrs. Redford and her staff provided job training, child care, and transportation for these women in their new lives.

Frankly, I was impressed. My mother's volunteer work consisted of volunteering to tell me how to live my life.

"Excuse me, Mom," Jack cut in when Mrs. Redford finally took a breath. "I haven't had a chance to introduce Kate to Dora." He turned to the maid, who stood silently by the kitchen. "Dora, this is my friend Kate Pride. Kate, Dora."

"Nice to meet you, Miss Pride," Dora said dutifully.

"You too," I said, feeling awkward.

"Dora made dinner. She's been with us for years. Wonderful cook," Mrs. Redford added, smiling as the older woman put out homemade apple cobbler. "Jackson? Diana Fife told me that your school has scheduled the vote on the flag. Is that so?"

He nodded. His mother patted her lips with her monogrammed napkin. "Interesting. Redford certainly is changing."

She didn't sound at all upset. I was pleasantly surprised by her attitude. "I think it's important for everyone to feel welcome in Redford, no matter how long their family has been here," I offered.

"Absolutely," Mrs. Redford agreed.

"The flag is so divisive," I said. "That's why we signed the petition."

Sally Redford regarded her son. "Jackson?"

"What?" His voice was pinched.

"I thought you said you weren't going to sign," she said calmly.

"I changed my mind."

"Yes, that's what I heard from Olivia Martin."

Jack's eyes went cold. "If Chaz's mom already told you, then why did you ask?"

"I was curious as to when you'd get around to informing me that you'd signed our name."

"I signed *my* name." Jack got up and began to clear dishes, so I stood to help him.

"Dora will get that," his mother objected.

"No," Jack said. "I'll do it."

He took the dessert plates from my hands and pivoted toward the kitchen without making eye contact with me. I sat back down. Okay, I shouldn't have opened my mouth. But I was so confused. If Jack's mother already knew he'd signed, why hadn't they discussed it before now? Besides, how could a woman who devoted so much of her life to helping people support a flag that represented the oppression of the ancestors of some of the very people she helped?

I knew I should say something to his mother. But what? Clearly the battle flag was off-limits. Maybe I could try: "Who did that to your hair?" I chose "Dinner was delicious" instead.

"I'm so glad you enjoyed it." She tapped one elegant finger on the tablecloth. "Kate, you seem like a lovely girl . . . "

There was *so* a "but" coming. I waited for her other pump to drop.

"And I know that at the moment Jackson is infatuated with you," she continued. "You're a very attractive young lady. Exotic, even, from Jack's point of view. I completely understand why he feels as he feels about you."

Huh. I'd certainly never been called exotic before. Maybe this wasn't going to be so bad. I smiled at her. "Thank you," I said.

"Why, when I was fourteen, I was madly in love with my riding instructor from Argentina! Can you imagine?" She laughed at the silly girl she'd been.

I felt like such an idiot, sitting there with a smile frozen on my face.

"I would be remiss as a mother, Kate, if I didn't warn you that there's no future in your relationship with my son. I don't want to see you get hurt."

I was speechless; my jaw flapping like an airborne fish sucking wind. The doorbell chimed and Mrs. Redford excused herself to get it. Jack came back and pulled me toward him for a hug. I yanked away from him.

He looked bewildered. "What?"

"Your mother . . . " I couldn't get the words out.

"What did she say to you?"

"Well, look who's here!" Mrs. Redford sang out as she sailed back into the room. Standing with her was a lovely, slender, auburn-haired woman. Next to the woman was her lovely, slender, red-haired daughter.

"Hey, Sara," Jack said awkwardly.

"Hey." She cut her eyes at me. "Kate." Sara Fife spit my name out like a curse, eyeing me as if I was roadkill.

Ever the gentleman, Jack introduced me to Mrs. Fife, then added, "I didn't know you were coming, Sara."

"Evidently not," she sniffed.

"Good to see you Mrs. Fife, Sara," Jack said, taking my arm. "Excuse us."

"Good to see you, too, Jackson," Mrs. Fife said as if I didn't exist. "We miss seeing you. Stop by soon."

I mustered every bit of politeness I could. "Thank you so much for a lovely dinner, Mrs. Redford." My oppositional subtext: Curl up and die, you witch.

We went out to my car. It had turned chilly, but not nearly as cold as it was inside. Jack wrapped his arms around me to warm me up.

"Your mom hates me."

"What'd she say to you?"

"Basically, that I'm a Yankee dirtbag who isn't good enough for you."

"My mother never said anything like that in her life."

"You're right. She's Southern. She said it in a way that made me want to say thank you."

He kissed my temple. "If you hadn't mentioned that I signed the—"

"But she already knew, Jack! She said so."

"Then there was no point in your bringing it up."

"Okay, I am totally confused," I admitted. "She already knew, and you *knew* she knew—"

"No, I guessed. She and Chaz's mother are friends. If she hadn't heard it from Olivia Martin, she'd have heard it from Crystal's mom, or Terry's mom, or—"

"So why didn't you just talk it over with her?"

"Kate. Did it seem to you like that conversation we just had in there was helpful?"

I bristled; it was if he was speaking to a child. "So, what, you play games with her instead of just getting things out in the open?"

"If that's what you want to call it."

"I call it not standing up for yourself," I said, my voice rising.

"Can we just drop it?"

"No. How long do you plan to hide who you really are?" I demanded. "Long enough to live out your mother's dreams? Go to The Citadel? Marry Sara?"

"I don't know, okay?" He was yelling now.

"No, it's not okay!"

We stared at each other across an abyss. For a long moment, the only sound was the last of the summer's crickets, the ones too hopeful or stubborn to die. But winter would come no matter what they did. Everything had a season. Nothing lasted forever; not even love. I thought about losing him and couldn't breathe.

"I'm not going to pretend I understand about you and your mom," I began, struggling to find the right words.

"But I shouldn't have told her you signed the petition without asking you first—even if she did already know about it," I admitted, my voice low. "It just kind of . . . came out. I'm sorry."

"Me too." He let his head fall back against the headrest and pulled me close.

"I wanted her to like me. I really, really did."

"It's okay. It doesn't matter." He stroked my hair. "She can't tell me who to love."

Love. It was the first time he'd used the word.

"You told me once that you didn't know what the word 'love' meant," I reminded him.

"That was then. This is now." Then he kissed me, and the rest of the world, including Sally Redford, didn't matter at all. It wasn't until I got home that I realized: Jack had introduced me to Dora, a woman old enough to be my grandmother, only by her first name.

13

Funny how I assumed Nikki's crusade was over. After all, she got what she wanted: a vote on the flag. Turned out her campaign had only started. It was no longer about getting a vote; now it was about convincing students *how* to vote. She hoped to use McSorley's month-long delay to rally people to the "right" side. Every day, she and her supporters set up a campaign table outside the cafeteria. JUST SAY NO buttons adorned jean jackets and backpacks. Meanwhile, quite a few people sported Confederate battle flag pins. With surprising magnanimity, McSorley permitted it, so long as everyone remained civil. He said we were learning to use the democratic process.

I was passing out buttons with Nikki in front of the cafeteria, and she was telling me about her weekend—she and her boyfriend, Michael, had bicycled from Redford to Nolensville—when Jack came by with Chaz and some of his other proflag friends. He separated from them and loped over, snaking an arm around my waist. "'Sup, ladies?"

"Just out here fighting the good fight, Jackson," Nikki said. "Button?"

He shook his head. "I don't like my clothes to speak for me, but thanks."

"Or maybe you just want to play both sides," Nikki suggested.

Which was sometimes my suspicion, too. But I stuck by my guy. "Everyone doesn't have to wear a button, Nikki," I said.

"In this town, the name Redford is almost as powerful as that flag," she declared, handing Jack a flyer. "Not taking a stand is tacit approval of the status quo. Think about it."

"Yes, ma'am," he teased, and stuck the leaflet in his pocket. "Kate, meet me after school by my car. I've got a surprise for you."

"Aren't we supposed to help paint the set?" I asked.

"That can wait." He nodded at Nikki, kissed me quickly, and left.

She got more flyers from the box. "So, you two happened fast."

I smiled. "Yeah."

"Dropping Sara Fife's ass makes me think Jack hasn't turned into a total wuss after all."

Odd remark. "What are you talking about?"

She handed a freshman a flyer. "We used to hang out."

"You and Jack? Did his mother know?"

"Sally Redford is . . . interesting. My mom does volunteer work with her at Redford Women United. It's a charity that—"

"Helps women get off welfare, I know all about it. I'm just surprised. She's so conservative, and your family is so liberal."

Nikki shrugged. "It's a good cause, what difference does it make?"

"Yeah, but his mother acts like the Confederate flag is her family crest."

"Things like that didn't separate us when we were kids. We all used to be friends. Believe it or not, even Sara."

"I guess this was pre–Crimson Maidens."

"Very," Nikki said. "Sara used to be the kind of girl who gives every kid in the class a valentine card so that no one feels left out. When I was a kid, I went to Redford House for Jack's birthday parties. Sara and Jack came to my birthday parties, too."

"Gee, lucky you. So what changed?"

"We grew up. Middle school, that's when all the parents freak."

"How does that make Jack a wuss?"

Nikki shrugged again. "When his mother changed the

rules—'Nicolette is a lovely girl, Jackson, but I'm sure she'd be more comfortable with her own people'—Jack folded like a taco."

"He was only a kid," I protested.

"Then. What's his excuse now? Everyone likes Jack. What's more, they respect him. If Jack Redford came out publicly against that flag, it would mean a lot, and he knows it. He's not a kid anymore."

• • •

Though mid-October, it was Indian-summer warm that afternoon when I met Jack in the parking lot after school. He rolled down the Jeep windows and pulled into the long line of cars snaking out onto the street. "So, what's the big surprise?" I asked.

"If I told you, it wouldn't be a surprise anymore."

Chaz's vintage red Mustang convertible was behind us, top down, music cranking, a small Confederate battle flag flapping from the antenna. Crystal sat next to him; Sara was in back with a guy I didn't recognize. As we pulled onto Franklin Road, Jack gave a friendly salute as the Mustang roared past us. Chaz saluted back. As he did, Sara's eyes caught mine for an instant.

I would be remiss as a mother, Kate, if I didn't warn you that there's no future in your relationship with my son.

According to Sally Redford, I was as inappropriate for Jack as the Argentinean riding instructor had been for her.

But Sara Fife was just right. It was obvious that Sara still thought so, too. All of which went under the heading Things I Don't Want to Think About.

Apropos of nothing, I said, "My dad had a Mustang just like Chaz's when my parents first got married."

Jack laughed. "My dad, too."

I couldn't picture Sally Redford tooling around in a hot convertible. The woman's hair hadn't moved in decades. "You never talk about your dad," I said.

"Not much."

"Does it make you too sad?"

"More like mad."

"Do you remember him?"

"Of course. I was almost eight when he died." I didn't press, but I could tell from the faraway look in his eyes that he was going back in time. "We did everything together. He was a terrific athlete. But what he loved most were ideas." Jack chuckled. "His idea of a bedtime story was telling me an Aesop's fable. Then we'd discuss the moral choices of the fox or the frog or whatever. His dream job was to teach philosophy."

"Did he ever do it?"

"No. He did what every Redford man had done before him, went to serve his country. Joined the air force. Five years later, we came back here to the family homestead. Dad started working on his doctorate in philosophy at Vanderbilt."

"I thought he died on a mission," I said hesitantly.

Jack's face hardened. "A damn training mission, in Alabama. He was in the reserves." He laughed bitterly. "Ever since it happened, my mother has talked about the 'nobility' of his sacrifice. But somehow it's lost on me."

Jack pushed a CD into the stereo and cranked it up, his way of saying he didn't want to talk about it anymore. I couldn't imagine how horrible it must have been to have his dad die when he was so little, and for no good reason at all. It was really too big for words, and I was glad to let the music save me.

Forty-five minutes later, Jack pulled off the state highway and followed a country road until a sign told us we were in Pulaski, Tennessee. And here, Jack unveiled his surprise: He'd arranged for me to interview Ron Bingham, the white separatist I'd read about in the newspaper. When I asked him how he'd pulled this off, he mumbled that he'd "made a few calls."

"You're sure he'll talk to me?" I asked.

"He talked to the *Tennessean,* he'll talk to you," Jack assured me.

The Bingham family lived in a small frame house just outside of town. There was a yard sign advertising his plumbing company. TRUST BINGHAM: FIFTY YEARS OF BEING THERE FOR YOU! A tire swing hung from an oak tree, and children's toys were scattered around the front yard.

Bingham's wife, Velma, answered the door. She wore yellow stretch pants and a floral shirt. Her blond hairdo featured upswept bangs like the spoiler on a hotrod. After a warm welcome, she led us into the living room, shooed away two little kids who were watching cartoons, and poured us glasses of lemonade. Ron would be home shortly, she said; he was over in Summertown working on a septic tank gone bad. She ushered us into his cramped office, instructing us to make ourselves at home until her husband arrived.

I looked around. Cheap wallpaper meant to look like wood paneling covered the walls, peeling in the corners. Over the desk was a framed newspaper clipping featuring a photo of a group of young white men. The caption identified them as members of WAR, the White Aryan Resistance.

"You know what the creepiest thing about this is?" I made a sweeping gesture with my hand. "It all looks so normal. The house. The kids . . . "

"Why, Jackson Redford, as I live and breathe!" a voice boomed.

I turned to see a man in his forties stride into the room. He was trim, with a movie-star grin under an orange Vols baseball cap. He wore battered jeans, work boots, and a denim shirt, its sleeves rolled up, with BINGHAM PLUMBING embroidered over the chest pocket.

"Ron Bingham." He pumped Jack's hand. "Call me Ron. It's an honor to meet you, boy. The Redford family is what Southern pride is all about."

So *that's* why he'd agreed to the interview. The name of the boy I loved had opened the door. Before I could digest that sickening tidbit of information, Bingham was introducing himself to me. When I shook his hand, I noticed the tattoo on his bicep of a white cross inside a black oval. At the center of the cross was a diamond; inside the diamond was a single backward apostrophe. I asked him about it and he eagerly lifted his sleeve higher to give me a better view.

"Cross of the Klan," he said proudly. He tapped the apostrophe mark. "That's a blood drop. Stands for the blood sacrificed for the white race."

All righty, then. I asked him if I could record our conversation; he readily agreed. I set the cassette recorder on the coffee table and took a seat on a battered wooden folding chair, which left Ron and Jack to share the brown leatherette couch.

"Any friend of Jackson Redford is a friend of mine," Ron told me, pulling off his baseball cap to reveal a blond crew cut. "So, what can I do you for, young lady?"

I wasn't sure how much Jack had told him, and I didn't want him to suspect my loathing for everything he believed in, lest he end the interview before it even began. "I'm trying to write about the Confederate flag and be fair to both sides," I explained. "I really would like to hear your point of view."

"Not a problem. You're Jack Redford's girl, that's enough of a recommendation for me." He crossed one leg over the other and jiggled it impatiently as he spoke. "Well, firstly, the big problem is they try to say the Confederate flag is the flag of racists."

"They?" I echoed.

"You know. The Mud People, Queer Nation, Communists, the Children of Satan Jews who control the media. The Godless. The mongrelized. There's a lot of 'em out there." He reeled this off like a grocery list.

His foot jiggled faster. I nodded as neutrally as I could.

Ron leaned toward me. "We dare to say aloud what others only think. We say: 'Rebels! Be proud! Stand tall! We are the South! Let us wave our pride!'"

"But there are lots of white Southerners who disagree with you, aren't there?"

"Well, I am of the opinion that they don't deserve the honor of that name. Do you understand what these so-called *enlightened* people want? They say they want to tear down our flag. But what they really want is an end to their own white race, and you can take that to the bank, young lady."

He stopped to shake his head at the horror of this notion before he went on. Then he slumped back and a grin split his face. "Sometimes I have to laugh. They don't even know. They are our best recruiters. You tell a young Southern white man you want to take his flag and his heritage away, know what he does? He runs right over to us." He held his arms wide. "And we say, 'Come on, son. You're one of us. This is your home.'"

He went on in this vein for a while, expounding on a litany of ills that faced America and how everyone other than his brand of white Christians was responsible for these ills. He said all this in a reasonable tone of voice, as if it actually made sense.

Finally, I asked him what he thought should happen to all the people who, in his estimation, were ruining America. His eyes twinkled as he spoke. "Do you know what the motto of the Confederate States of America was, Kate?"

I allowed that I did not.

Ron cocked his head toward Jack. "Ask your boyfriend."

"Deo Vindice," Jack said.

Ron's grin widened. "Yes-siree Bob. *Deo Vindice.* With God As Our Defender. This was the Confederate motto. This is the motto we live by today."

"I see," I said. "So God is on your side."

"You make sure your tape gets this," Ron said, leaning toward my cassette recorder. "Make no mistake about it. The white Anglo-Saxons are the *true* Israelites. We *will* smite the enemies of God's chosen people. And then the world shall be returned to our righteous hands."

14

If football was Redford's unofficial religion, then the home games with Franklin West and South Columbia High were holy days. They were the Rebels' chief rivals for the division title and the subject of conversation everywhere I went.

The game with Franklin West came first. That Friday evening, my mom was in Nashville, doing research for a freelance magazine piece about the city's best day spas. Portia and I were waiting for our respective rides to the game. I was going with Jack, of course. Portia was going with her friend Cassidy, accompanied by Cassidy's mother.

My sister kept checking her reflection in the hallway

mirror. She was wearing a dainty pink sweater set that she said was similar to one owned by Madison Honeywell, fashion arbiter of Redford East Middle School—and a touch of pink lip gloss. "But this ponytail makes my face look fat," she declared.

"No, it doesn't." I didn't look up from the pages I was reading—my transcript of Ron Bingham's interview. It was like a terrible car accident. One part of you wants to look away and not see something so horrible, but another part of you is fascinated.

"Kate, should I cut my hair?" Portia asked.

"Hey, I love your hair, sugarplum," my father drawled from his beloved Barcalounger. On his lap was the Styrofoam container of deep-fried catfish takeout that my mother had forbidden in a preemptive strike against high cholesterol.

Portia looked aghast. "Daddy, you had a Southern accent just now."

"Danged if I didn't." My father grinned wildly.

She looked even more horrified. "Okay, no offense, Daddy, but you sound retarded. If Cassidy comes in, please don't say anything dumb."

He wiped tartar sauce from his chin. "Well, hush my mouth."

"Kate, make him stop."

Before I could respond, there was a loud honk. Portia peeked out from the living room curtains and gasped. "Kate. Look!"

I got up to look outside. There was a blue Lexus in our driveway. Cassidy sat in front, next to her mother. Two boys were in the back.

"So?"

"That's Barney, the boy I told you about," she hissed. "And his friend Alan. I didn't know they were riding with us. What should I do?"

"Get your purse. Go outside. Get in the car."

"Squished in the backseat with *two boys?*"

"What two boys?" my father called.

Portia's eyes pleaded with me for rescue.

"Just some boys in her class," I said.

Dad frowned as Cassidy's mom honked again. "You're much too young to date, Porsche."

"It's not a date," I assured my father.

Portia mouthed "Thank you" and reached for her purse. I told her she looked great and gave her a quick hug.

"Hold on, Porsche." My father stopped his movie. "I want to meet these people."

"Daddy, no. You can't! Daddy—"

Too late. A moment later, he was out the front door, red-faced Portia trailing behind him. They nearly collided with Jack, who sidestepped them on his way up the walk. He came through the screen door and gave me a hug. "Your sister looks as if she's about to face a firing squad," he joked.

"First kinda-sorta date," I explained.

"You remember yours?"

"Sure. When I was six, we took a school trip to the Bronx Zoo. I told David Levine that if he didn't hold my hand, I'd beat him up. Does that count?"

"Absolutely." Jack saw the transcript pages strewn across the coffee table. "So, how's the writing going?"

Dangerous question. If anything should have been the catalyst for me to write a decent play, it was my interviews with Ron Bingham and Malik El Baz. I was certainly following Marcus's decree that you can't write what you don't know. Well, now I knew a lot. That very morning, I'd tried again. Nothing. Portia could have written a better play. I didn't know why I was stuck. And I didn't want to admit it, not even to Jack.

"Slow," I said evasively.

"When can I read it?"

"I'll let you know."

"Well, when you're ready, Miss Bright is ready," Jack reminded me.

Maybe it was because the school was buzzing about the upcoming vote that Nikki had casually mentioned in drama class that I was working on a play about the flag furor. I'd expected Miss Bright to react badly. Instead, she'd asked me its title. When I said *Black and White and Redford All Over,* there were appreciative murmurs. It must have impressed Miss Bright, too, because she said she thought it was wonderful that both of our plays were "timely and relevant." Then Savy Leeman suggested that when I had a draft done, the class should do a reading. Miss Bright agreed. I'd feigned great enthusiasm while knowing that at the rate I was going, I'd be ready for that reading sometime in the next millennium.

Jack thumbed through my transcript of Bingham's interview. "This guy is a piece of work."

"No kidding. Scary that he thinks, deep down, you're one of his boys."

"I know."

I fiddled with the back on an earring. "Jack, no one in your family was ever . . . ?"

"In the Klan?" He looked up, and I nodded. "My father wasn't. My grandfather wasn't. Beyond that, I don't know."

How could he say that so casually? Redford ancestors could have been running around in white sheets; Jack didn't know. Worse, he didn't seem to care.

"Don't you think—" I began.

"What I *think* is that both of us think too much." He put the transcript back on the table and playfully pulled me to my feet. "Come on. You are about to be initiated into a top-secret, Redford tradition known only to the few, the proud, and the desperate to win the Franklin West game."

He looked so cute. And he was right; I needed a break. "Okay. You talked me into it. I am in your hands."

"Really? Well, that could make life very interesting."

His lips were inches from mine when my father came inside, his shoulders drooping. "It's official. I've lost my youngest daughter to preteendom." He trudged back to the Barca and sank into the Naugahyde. "It's all downhill from here. Don't mind me. I'll just watch my movie and dream of being Mel Gibson while my arteries harden. Have fun at the game."

• • •

A half hour later, the high beams of Jack's Jeep cut the darkness like twin light swords as we bumped along a gravel path. From my house, he'd driven back toward Redford House. Then, instead of taking the private drive to the front gate, he'd turned onto this country lane.

"So where does this top-secret thing take place?" I asked Jack after a nasty jolt pitched me against him.

"You'll see."

"Is all this your property?"

"For better or worse, in the family since 1852." He gripped the vibrating steering wheel as the lane wound to the right. High corn on both sides of us gave way to woods. Finally, we came to a small clearing. Jack pulled alongside a parked Volvo and turned off the engine.

"This is it," he announced as the gloom of night swallowed us. He reached into the back, found two flashlights, and handed one to me.

I flicked it on and aimed the light upward from my chin. "No one returns from the Cult of the Sacrificial Volvo," I intoned, adding my best "Mwa-ah-ah!" vampire laugh.

He winced. "You're right. You really can't act."

"Thanks!" I swatted his butt as we got out of the car. But no amount of prodding on my part would get him to explain where we were or what we were doing. He aimed his flashlight and led the way along a narrow path through the woods. Finally, we emerged in another clearing, smaller than the first one. I swung my flashlight around to find that we were standing on neatly trimmed grass edged by tall rhododendrons. In a corner of the clearing, I saw a square granite building. We trained our lights on its solid brass door.

"What is it?" I asked as we got close.

Suddenly there was a terrible wail from inside whatever the building was, and two spectral zombies leaped out at us, arms flailing. I screamed, jumped backward, and fell on my ass.

That's when I heard a girl's gleeful voice. "Gotcha, gotcha, gotcha!"

I propped myself up on my elbows, pretty sure I recognized it. "Tisha?"

"Welcome to the crypt of the living dead!" she hooted. She, Terry, and my boyfriend all stood over me, laughing.

"You scared the crap out of me!"

"Tell you what, I'd pay to see that again on videotape," Jack said, extending a hand to hoist me up while Terry retrieved my flashlight for me.

"Very funny." I brushed myself off and shined my beam again at the stone building. "Is that thing really a crypt?"

Jack put his hand solemnly on his heart. "Final resting place for generation upon generation of the Redford dearly departed."

A chill chased up my spine. "You mean this is your family's mausoleum?"

Tisha linked arms with him playfully. "Also the official site of The Ritual, wherein we invoke the spirits of rebels past to bring good fortune to Rebels present."

Jack gestured toward the open door and looked at me. "Madam?"

I held back, my voice low. "Your *dad* is buried here. "

"My dad was Redford High's starting quarterback," Jack said, smiling. "Believe me, he's into it."

A Coleman lantern illuminated a blanket and picnic basket on a bare marble floor. Everyone plopped down on the blanket, so I did, too. Terry took foil-wrapped paper plates from the picnic basket and handed them around. I peeked under the foil. There was a big pinkish thing, little fried-looking things and a pile of light brown curly things. Ick. "I don't think this restaurant is in the Michelin guide," I said.

"No dissing the cuisine, Jersey," Terry warned. "Now, listen up." He pointed to items on the plate. "You got your salt-cured country ham, your pork rinds, and your week-old hush puppies—fried corn bread they throw to the hounds to shut 'em up."

"Maybe we could just summon some hungry dogs," I suggested hopefully.

"No way," Tisha said. "We've eaten this same noxious pregame meal before the Franklin home game for the last three years. And we won 'em all."

"Coincidence?" Jack asked, wriggling his eyebrows. "I think not."

"You don't mess with tradition," Terry declared, crunching into a pork rind.

"Eat up," Jack told me cheerfully, popping a piece of country ham into my mouth. It tasted like a salt lick. "The football gods don't like leftovers."

They insisted that I eat everything on my plate. Somehow, I did, which earned me a round of applause. We were joking and laughing, and I realized that for the first time, I was actually having fun with Jack's friends.

Tisha took a small flask from her pocket. "And now, the official Tennessee moonshine invocation." She swigged and passed the flask to Terry, who did the same and gave it to me. I took a sip—and choked, much to their amusement, but that stuff is strong—then handed it to Jack, who rose, flask in hand.

"Dear Lord," he began. "We four unworthy sinners humbly invoke the spirit of Rebels past. We ask that You guide many touchdown passes into the arms of our brother Chaz and light the way for the Redford Rebels to victory against the godless Franklin West Warriors. Can I get an amen?"

"Amen!" we chorused.

Jack emptied the flask onto the floor. "The ghosts are now officially sated," he declared.

"Good," Tisha said. "Because the stone under here is so cold that my ass is numb. You wanna come warm it up, big guy?"

Terry was more than willing. "We'll catch up with y'all

at the game. Go Rebels!" With a rousing Rebel yell, they ran out the door.

I leaned my head on Jack's lap. "I'm having fun. In a sick kind of way. Why aren't your other friends here?"

"We used to have a few more people. But now Chaz is a starter on the team, so he can't be here—"

"And Sara's probably been a cheerleader since she could swing a pom-pom," I guessed, then looked around. "This place really doesn't creep you out?"

He stroked my hair. "Used to. Remember I told you about that time Chaz and I ditched school to go fishing?"

"And you had to apologize to, like, everyone in town?"

"Right," he laughed. "My mother said I'd 'besmirched the family name.' She also made me come out here and clear brush for the entire weekend. Then I had to copy the name and date of every set of bones in this crypt onto a family tree. She checked it for accuracy, too."

"She couldn't just ground you?"

He chuckled. "Not Sally Redford's style. At first I was sure some ghoul would rise up and smite me for my wicked ways. When that didn't happen, I started to like being out here. After that, I came on my own every now and then."

"Why?"

"To daydream. I spent one entire year imagining I was Superman. Then I changed to Spider-Man."

"Cooler outfit." I sat up and looked around. The walls were lined with coffins slid into granite slots, one atop another, like some kind of macabre filing system. A brass plate on the end sticking out gave names, dates, and epitaphs.

"Where's your dad buried?" I asked him.

He cocked his head toward the vault closest to the door. "Every male descendant of Eustis Redford rests here."

That's when I noticed the empty slot above his father. For him.

I tried to keep my tone light. "You will spend nine or ten decades as America's finest actor and die in your sleep at the age of one hundred and ten."

"What if that's not the right thing, Kate?" He made a sweeping gesture with his hand. "All of them, every single one, served. You think they'd tell me, 'You want to be an actor? Go on then, son. Be whoever you want to be.'"

• • •

Jack steered the Jeep back the way we'd come. But at a fork in the lane, he veered left. "Detour. You mind?"

"We'll miss the kickoff."

"This is more important."

What could be more important to him than football? We bumped down what looked like a cart path overgrown with weeds. Finally, the headlights illuminated a tumbledown cabin nestled in the woods. Next to it were the exposed foundations of some other small structures. Jack's headlights beamed at the cabin.

"Where are we?" I asked. But suddenly, like a fist to the gut, I knew. It was just as Mrs. Augustus had told me. "It's slave quarters."

He nodded. "Most rich Southerners had slaves. At the start of the Civil War, there were as many black slaves in this county as there were free whites."

"Unreal."

"That time my mother made me write down the names in the mausoleum? She had me copy them into the back of the family Bible. The names of Major General Redford's slaves are listed there. All forty-two of them."

He kept his car lights on so we could see, and we went into the cabin. It was empty. I wondered who had lived there, who had suffered or died there. "Your mother should tear this down, Jack."

"My great-granddaddy did, the others. But not this one."

"Why?"

"Tearing it down wouldn't change what happened." He ran a finger along the rough-hewn logs that formed the cabin walls. "I never brought anyone here, Kate. Until now. Not even Sara."

"Why?"

"Too close to the bone, maybe. Besides, her family has its own skeletons rattling around in the battlefield cemetery. But with you . . . " He puffed out some air and ran his hand through his hair. "People throw around the words 'I love you' until they don't mean anything. I never said it to anyone until I said it to you. But what I feel is bigger than . . . It's like the words can't even hold it all."

I wrapped my arms around his neck. "Me too," I whispered.

"So I want you to know, Kate. Everything."

I nodded.

"All my dreaming . . . wanting to be an actor . . . someone I'm not . . . maybe it's just fear that I can't measure up."

"I don't believe that."

"I'm ashamed that my ancestors owned slaves. But that doesn't mean I'm not still proud of them, because I am. They were honorable men, for a different time. And they put love of country ahead of whatever they wanted for themselves. Can you understand that? Can you?"

This was where Jack came from, where turning away from service was like turning your back on the family faith. I got the unspoken message: If I couldn't accept that, then I couldn't really accept him.

15

R-E-B-E-L
THAT'S THE REDFORD REBEL YELL!
V-I-C-T-O-R-Y
THAT'S THE REDFORD REBEL CRY!

The Rebels beat Franklin West by three touchdowns. Chaz's house was packed for the victory party, and the spirit was infectious. A boy standing on the living room couch led us in a cheer so loud they must have heard it back in Englecliff. I shouted along with everyone else, figuring what's the harm? After all, the way JUST SAY NO buttons were outnumbering battle flags, it looked like Redford High School would soon have a new team name and emblem. Besides, football was a unifying force. All the black players were at the party with their girlfriends, and they were bellowing along with everyone else.

Sara was there. She ignored me. But Jack's other friends were coming around. Tisha enlisted my help with a drunken girl, hysterical over a fight with her boyfriend. After the girl cried herself out, we found her a ride home. Even Chaz made an effort. After I congratulated him on the touchdown pass he'd caught and made reference to how it must have been divinely inspired, he told me that if I made "his boy Jackson" happy, by God, he was happy for both of us. Then, to Jack's delight, he swallowed me up in a bear hug.

Clearly, Chaz was starting to accept me. I thought maybe I should interview him for my play. I'd done a half dozen more interviews. Meanwhile, the local media began to cover the upcoming vote. Waiting for the Strikers game to start on Saturday, I read the *Tennessean*. It was full of vociferous letters to the editor about Redford, some for the flag, some against it.

Saturday night, Jack and I stayed late at Peace Inn. Around two in the morning a teenage girl with a black eye showed up. I called the police, showed her where the shower was, got her some clean clothes from the clothes box, and found her an empty bed. When she took off her jacket, I saw she had the same tattoo on her bicep as Ron Bingham.

The next day, we were at the Peace Inn again, helping

the latest round of temporary residents prepare a spaghetti lunch, when Jack's mother appeared on the local TV news. Representing the Redford Historical Association, she told a reporter that the Confederate battle flag had never been intended as a symbol of racism, and that bigots had simply usurped it. Half the kids we were with were black; they snickered at the TV as they cooked.

Very late that afternoon, Jack introduced me to yet another of his favorite spots—the top of Redford's water tower. The trick, he said, was not to look down as you climbed. But I was still petrified. Once we'd reached the flat summit, though, it was worth it. The setting sun shimmered on the horizon, and the late-October air had a definite chill. When Jack held me, I felt as if we were suspended in some magical place where only the two of us existed.

Maybe it was that magic that made me start to speculate about our future. I thought aloud about how next year I'd return to Englecliff High as a senior and have my shot at Showcase. How Jack could start his freshman year at Juilliard. Then, after I graduated, I'd go to NYU, and we'd get an apartment together in Manhattan. I'd write plays and Jack would be in them. We'd be so happy.

He didn't say a word. Which made me think that maybe I was being incredibly presumptuous. "I swear, I'm not trying to talk you into anything," I added hastily. "But I don't think doing the right thing . . . should have to mean giving up your dreams."

He gazed into the sunset, as if seeing our future just beyond the horizon. He said he'd make his mother understand that his dreams were different from hers. He said so long as we had each other, we had everything. He said he loved me. The sun disappeared, night fell, and he kissed me until the light of all the stars was inside me. Together, we were above the fray. We were invincible.

• • •

It happened three days later, on Wednesday.

If I hadn't promised Tisha the history notes she'd missed because of a doctor's appointment, I would never have known. Her locker was in the high school's new wing. So when the final bell rang, I trucked down there—the opposite direction from where I usually met Jack after school. In this wing, on Wednesdays, representatives from various colleges and universities set up shop. Seniors could get excused from last period to go hear the rap on why they should attend whatever school was recruiting that day.

I'd already passed two classrooms filled with students and recruiters when what I'd seen on an easel outside one of them registered in my mind. I stopped, then backtracked. There was the hand-lettered sign. THE CITADEL, CHARLESTON, SC.

I peered inside. Two young men in crisp gray military uniforms stood in front of a white board, speaking to a small group of seniors. Chaz was front and center. And next to him was Jack. The boy who had spun dreams with me of a life together in New York.

Jack the fraud. Jack the liar.

The recruiters must have just been finishing, because kids were standing and gathering their books. I watched Chaz approach the men to ask a question; one of them gave an animated answer. Then Chaz and Jack headed toward the door. And me.

It was obvious from Jack's expression that he hadn't planned for me to see him there. Chaz, who sported a Confederate flag pin on his shirt, seemed oblivious to the tension. "Yo, Kate-date. You're in luck. We just found out that Yankee girlfriends don't need a passport at The Citadel dances."

I didn't laugh.

"These are the jokes, girl!" He nudged me playfully. Finally, he seemed to get that something was amiss, said he'd catch Jack later, and took off.

Jack looked resigned and leaned against the lockers, wagging his fingers toward himself. "Okay. Come on. Give me your best shot."

Give me your best shot? Like I was his punishment, his jailer? I turned on my heel and strode away from him. He caught up with me. "Hey, come on. Don't be that way."

"No, *you* come on, Jack. Everything you said—"

"Everything *you* said," he countered.

"But you agreed with me. You said so! You said . . . Just forget it." I gritted my teeth and quickened my pace until I pushed out the heavy front doors into a cold, gloomy afternoon.

Jack kept up with me as I hurried toward my car. "Would you just stop? Please?"

I didn't, and I wouldn't look at him. "Why did you lie to me? That's all I want to know."

"I didn't. . . . I was . . . I want all those things we talked about, Kate. But sometimes you can't have what you want, no matter how much you want it."

"You should have just told me the truth." It was drizzling now; I pulled my jacket closer and pressed the remote to unlock my car doors.

"Kate." He slipped between the door and me. As I tried to muscle past him, the skies opened up; cold rain sheeted down on us.

"Get out of my way."

He didn't budge. "Not until we talk about this."

"There's nothing to talk about. You'll tell me whatever I want to hear, I'll believe you, and we'll just keep going through this. You're a Redford. You'll do the right thing. Go to The Citadel. Marry the right girl. Lead the right life."

"Kate—"

"And don't tell me how noble it is," I ranted, oblivious to the elements. "Because that's just an excuse. It's not going into service you're afraid of, Jack. It's not even going to war. It's living your own life."

The fight seemed to go out of him. He stepped aside

and let me get into my car. As I drove away, he was still standing there. And I couldn't tell where the rain left off and my tears began.

• • •

I curled into a ball on my cushioned window seat under the eaves and rocked to the rhythm of the rain. I told my parents I wasn't feeling well and didn't go down for dinner. After a while, Portia tiptoed in with a tray of tea and cookies. My father brought me an afghan and kissed my forehead. Finally, my mother made her appearance. She asked if I'd had a fight with Jack. I said I didn't want to talk about it. She told me that she loved me; she was there if I needed her. On her way out, she fluffed the pillows on my bed, centering her favorite: THE PURPOSE OF LIFE IS A LIFE OF PURPOSE. "Maybe writing would help you get in touch with your feelings," she said.

She didn't understand. I couldn't possibly write. I was hollow, bruised, and at the same time, numb. Without Jack, all color was bleached from the world, all happiness. I fell asleep by the window to the staccato tattoo of raindrops on glass.

Tick, tick, tick. It's over. It's over. It's over. *Tick. Tick. Tick.*

Swimming up from my dream, I thought how much time there was between the drops, and how heavy they sounded. *Tick. Tick. Tick.* Not raindrops, my mind said. Sleet.

But this was Tennessee in October. It couldn't be sleet. I opened my eyes. The room was inky black. I was curled into an impossible position on the window seat and had a terrible crick in my neck.

Plink!

Something smacked the glass, hard. I jumped. And I realized it wasn't rain or sleet; what had just tapped the glass was a pebble. I yanked the window open and peered out. Jack was down in my yard, peering up. My heart wanted to rocket out the window and into his arms. But my brain said: Don't be a fool. He'll hurt you all over again.

He motioned for me to come down. I pushed into some flip-flops, grabbed a sweater, and ran downstairs through my silent house. The kitchen clock read ten past one. I went into the yard, vowing to harden my heart.

"You almost broke my window." I rubbed my arms, and my words formed clouds in front of me. For the first time since I'd left New Jersey, I could see my breath against the chill of the air.

He shoved his hands in his pockets. "I didn't think I should call this late."

"What do you want?"

"I . . . " He stopped, then started again. "My mother has terrible insomnia."

I stared at him blankly. "Gee. Good to know."

"That didn't come out the way I—" He ran his hand through his hair. "This afternoon . . . after you left, I walked around in the storm, didn't know where I was going. I ended up in the Confederate cemetery by the golf course. I started reading the headstones. Lots of those boys weren't any older than me, dead before they ever lived. When I thought about losing you, I felt like I was already one of them."

"Those are just words." A fist squeezed my chest. "You don't know what you want, Jack."

"I know I don't want to go to The Citadel."

My anger flared. "Gimme a break. Nine hours ago, you were meeting with their recruiter!"

"I didn't have to attend that meeting. There's a Redford Hall there. I could flunk out of high school and run around in lipstick, I'd still get in."

"So why did you show up?"

"Because I said I would. Besides, they'd have called my mother in a New York minute if I hadn't showed up."

I felt so tired. "You're never going to tell your mother you don't want to go there. I never should have expected that you would."

"Kate, I already told her."

I couldn't have heard him correctly. "You *told* her?"

"Just now. That's what I meant about insomnia. She was in the study, reading. I told her everything."

"What's 'everything'?" I asked cautiously.

"That I e-mailed the admissions office to say I won't be attending. That I've filled out an application for a regional audition for Juilliard."

Wow. For a long moment I was speechless. All his

switching back and forth was dizzying. Part of me was happy, but part was skeptical. Because it was just like after we'd argued at the mall. It was as if I was pushing him to change, and he was complying.

"Are you sure that's what you want?" I finally asked. "If it's because of your mother—"

"I didn't make the decision to spite her. And I didn't do it for you."

"So if I lived in, like, upper Mongolia, you'd still want to go to school in New York?"

A smile tugged at the corners of his mouth. "Did I ever tell you that you're a pain in the ass?"

"It's a gift."

"I told my mother one other thing," Jack said. He took a step closer to me. "I told her I love a girl named Kate Pride. And nothing and no one can change that. Ever."

His arms went around me, and we stood there, heart to heart. That I had almost lost him seemed impossible, and at the same time, too true. I wanted to be inside his skin. To breathe the air he breathed. To never, ever let go.

Silently, we went up to my room and lay down on my bed. Any other night, in a boxing match between caution and lust, lust would have won in an early-round TKO. But this wasn't any other night. We were a shattered vase, pieces glued back together. So we lay atop the covers, fully clothed, and held each other carefully, as if passion might cause the jagged fault lines to splinter again.

16

Jack left just before dawn. The next day, at school, he was different; quieter, with less ease to his gait. I told myself he was just stressed. Even Chaz, not one to pick up on subtleties, asked Jack if he was okay. At lunch, we took a silent walk on one of the trails that wound around Redford Hill. Crimson and gold leaves pirouetted down from the trees, and I thought how sad it was that they were most beautiful just before they died.

After school, the cast of Miss Bright's play did an off-book run-through in the theater. Attendance was mandatory. We went and applauded politely at the end, but a couple of months of rehearsal had not improved the text.

Not that I had any right to dis her work. Unlike me, she'd actually written something.

By unspoken agreement, Jack and I went to my house—he hadn't seen his mother since their midnight showdown and didn't want to see her now. In the Jeep, we didn't turn on the radio or a CD. We just drove. When we turned onto Beauregard Lane, there was a gray Cadillac parked in my driveway. "That's my mom's car," Jack said, pulling up to the curb.

"What's she doing here?"

"I don't know."

My mom's Saturn was in the driveway, too. Which meant our moms were in there together. Whatever was happening could not possibly be good. "Let's go," I said impetuously.

"Where?"

"Memphis. Hanoi. Jupiter." I stared hard at the front door. Maybe if I really concentrated, I could divine the conversation going on inside.

"Obviously, they're talking about us," Jack said. "We should go in."

I bit at a cuticle. "When did you get so brave?"

"When did you get so weenie?" he shot back. Of course, he knew that comment guaranteed I'd get my butt out of his Jeep.

Our moms were in the formal living room, which we hardly ever used. Mine sat on the couch in worn jeans and a Rutgers T-shirt. Sally Redford, whose hair looked like it hadn't moved since the last time I'd seen her, was perched ramrod straight on the paisley chair. She wore gray wool pants, heels, and a peach silk blouse. Steaming cups of coffee and some pastries were on the coffee table between them.

My mom filled us in: Sally Redford had called to ask if she might stop over with some home-baked pastries as a belated welcome to Redford gift.

"Mom, what are you really doing here?" Jack asked.

"I was just getting to that, Jackson."

I sat on the arm of the couch near my mom. Jack stood by the wall in the demilitarized zone, halfway between our mothers. Without further niceties, Sally Redford got down to the real deal: her son and me. His "stunning" midnight announcement. His "legacy," and how I did not fit into it. My mom listened intently without interrupting.

When Mrs. Redford finally reached the end of her soliloquy, my mother took a contemplative sip of coffee before she spoke. "Interesting. Is there a point?"

Jack jumped in. "No, Mrs. Pride, I don't think there is." He turned to his mother. "I told you, Mom. I've already made my decision."

Mrs. Redford offered a tight-lipped smile. "Do you know what my greatest disappointment is, Jackson? That I apparently have failed so miserably in how I raised you. I feel I should apologize to your father for the mess I've made of things."

"This isn't about you," Jack said wearily.

"Of course it's about me," Sally Redford insisted. "We're talking about family, honor, and responsibility. Like it or not, Jackson, I'm the only family you have."

"Mrs. Redford." My mom set down her coffee. Her

voice was calm, but I could see fireworks behind her eyes. "Your son is a terrific young man. I'm sure your husband would be proud of how you've raised him. But as far as where he goes to college or what he studies, don't you think that should be Jack's choice?"

"And I'm sure you understand that is between me and my son, Mrs. Pride," Sally Redford said in honeyed tones.

"I quite agree. But you came here and made me a part of it."

"You do see that Jackson never would have made this choice if not for your daughter." Mrs. Redford turned to me. "I blame myself more than I blame you, Kate."

"Leave Kate out of this," Jack snapped.

"My dear son, you have made that impossible. Believe me, I know how seductive a beautiful young girl can be. I used to be one."

My face burned. "I didn't . . . *seduce* your son, Mrs. Redford."

"If the next step in your plan is to get pregnant, by quote unquote 'mistake—'"

"I would never . . . We're not even—" I stuttered.

"You don't owe her an explanation," Jack told me.

My mother stood, a clear indicator that as far as she was concerned, this conversation was over. "You obviously know nothing about my daughter or the kind of person she is."

"I don't doubt her attributes," Mrs. Redford said, also

rising. "I just doubt them for my son. And I won't let his future be compromised by a high school crush. I have to insist that Kate and Jack not see each other anymore."

"You expect them to just accept that?" my mother asked, incredulous.

"Parenting isn't a popularity contest, Mrs. Pride."

"Enough!" Jack exclaimed, holding his palm up. "Stop. Both of you just . . . stop." He took a deep breath and then exhaled slowly. "Mrs. Pride, I'm sorry my mother came here with this. She shouldn't have. Mom, I'm sorry if you disagree with my decisions. But if they're mistakes, they're *my* mistakes, not yours."

His mother was unmoved. "Jackson, if I have to send you to military school to keep you two apart, I'll do it."

"You can't do that!" I protested.

"Don't presume to tell me what I can and can't do, young lady."

"She's not telling you," Jack said, voice steely, eyes cold. "I am. I love Kate. And she loves me. Maybe if you'd ever allowed yourself an honest emotion that wasn't colored by some . . . some antiquated concept of the right thing to do, you'd be happy for me. I wish you were. But even if you're not, it won't change how I feel. Or what I do." He reached for my hand. "Come on."

For the first time, his mother's façade seemed to slip a little. "Where do you think you're going?"

"I don't know, Mom. But right now, anywhere's a better place to be."

17

So. The battle lines were drawn. I thought it was incredibly unfair that his mother had rejected me, but I was proud of Jack for standing up to her. He assured me that her threat to send him to military school wasn't serious. She wasn't about to pull her Redford son out of Redford High, if only because it would reflect badly on her parenting. Besides, he'd turn eighteen in four months, and then she couldn't call the shots anymore.

I didn't doubt that Jack loved his mother. She was smart and interesting and she adored him. After his father's death, she'd raised him alone. Sitting there on the banks of the Harpeth, he told me more about her. How the Redford family fortune had doubled in the past ten years because of her shrewd investments. How she gave away vast amounts of money to worthy causes and worked harder for free at her charities than most people did at their paying jobs. Because of Sally Redford, scores of women on welfare had reclaimed their lives.

I was impressed. Politics aside, in a different situation I would have admired her. But I was who I was, and that changed everything. Jack had promised his mother he'd accompany her to a Vanderbilt University Children's Hospital fund-raiser that night, and being Jack, he wouldn't go back on his word.

Before dinner my mom told my dad all about Mrs. Redford's last stand and decreed we wouldn't ruin our meal by rehashing it. So instead, Portia prattled on about Barney, her first boyfriend. (Of course, knowing that our parents would disapprove, Portia didn't actually use the word "boyfriend" but rather the code phrase "this guy in my class.") Barney was evidently writing a fan-fiction prequel to Harry Potter. My parents listened to Portia's plot summary as if Barney had already won a Pulitzer.

"Does he get good grades?" my mother asked, sipping her iced tea.

Portia nodded. "Straight A's. He's supersmart, Mom."

My dad tugged gently on Portia's ponytail. "So are you, kiddo."

"Dad!" she protested.

"Friends are important," my mom continued. "But grades are—"

"More important," Portia finished, rolling her eyes. "You've said it like a million times. You know, you should try using reverse psychology, and say that *boys* are the most important thing in the universe, so that I'd say they *aren't.*"

"Would that work?" my mom asked wryly.

"I suppose not," honest Portia replied. "And studies have shown that repetition reinforces behavior."

My mom chuckled. "Well, good for me then, for staying on message." She raised her eyebrows at me, a not-so-subtle reminder that regardless of what was happening with Jack, the Life of Purpose thing still applied to me, too. "How's your play coming, Kate?"

"Oh, you know . . . ," I said evasively.

The truth was—it was excruciating to admit, even to myself—I still had not written a single scene. At my angriest, I blamed Marcus. He'd accused me of writing fast-food theater. I'd internalized the message. Now, not only were my efforts not good, they weren't even funny. I was starting to suspect that I didn't have enough talent to write what Marcus would consider a real play.

I wasn't ready to give up, though. Disgusted by my own lack of progress, I pushed back from the table with new determination and went upstairs to gather my laptop and bulging folder of interview transcripts. Hoping for inspiration, I drove over to the brand-new Starbucks and set up at an outdoor table in sight of the Civil War monument.

And I tried. I really tried. But an hour later, when I stopped to read what I'd written, I wanted to cry. Because it was dreadful.

"Hi."

Startled, I looked up. Standing by my table was the last person I'd expect to see greeting me: Sara Fife. She took in my coffee, my computer, my notes. Then she ignored them. "Mind if I sit down?"

"I'm kind of busy, actually." I closed the scene I'd been writing without saving it to my hard drive. It didn't matter. It was hardly worth saving.

"I won't stay long." She sat across from me, hands wrapped around an oversized plastic cup. "It is a sad fact of life that Redford, Tennessee, is the last place on the planet to get a Starbucks."

"I thought you loved Redford."

"I do. It's a sadder fact of life how pathetically happy I am about it. I'm addicted to these." She picked up her Iced Caffè Mocha and smiled. "So, working on your play?"

I took a mental step backward. "How did you know about that?"

"My friend Pansy is in your drama class. She said you're writing about the flag. It's not a secret, is it?"

"No," I said warily.

"You aren't going to make all of us sound like Jared Boose, are you?"

"Definitely not."

"Good. Because he is quite the singular sensation."

"Yeah, I kind of got that. I've been interviewing people on both sides. Trying to learn . . ."

"So, what'd you learn?"

What *had* I learned? I thought a moment. Even Mrs. Augustus had admitted to me that though she no longer flew that flag, she still loved it. And Mrs. Augustus was no racist. "I guess what I've learned is that while racists may love that flag, not everyone who loves it is a racist."

"Good for you." I thought I saw a new respect in her eyes. "Can I read what you've written?"

Which would be exactly nothing. "I don't like anyone to read my stuff when it's still in progress."

She nodded and sipped her drink. "Especially not me, right?"

I decided to go for honest, because what the hell. "Right."

"Yeah. I don't blame you." She stared into her cup. "There's something I've been wanting to say to you."

What? You stole my boyfriend? I waited for the grenade I was certain she was about to lob.

"Jackson was my first love," she said softly. "I thought we'd always be together. Then he met you, and everything changed." She finally raised her eyes to me. "I despised you at first. I admit it. But not anymore."

"You don't?" I asked cautiously.

"I will always care about Jackson. I guess what I learned about myself is that I care about him enough to want him to be happy, even if he isn't happy with me. Does that make any sense?"

"In a way-more-mature-than-me way, yeah."

She laughed ruefully. "Maturity hasn't been my strong suit in the past. I'm sure I have a ways to go yet."

God. Like so much else about Redford, I had completely misjudged her. "I'm so sorry," I blurted out.

"For what?"

"For all the mean things I thought about you."

"Ditto." She held her hand out to me. I shook it. She pushed out of her chair. "Well, good luck with your play. I admire writers so much. Every time we get a creative writing assignment, I just wilt. I'll see you around."

"Bye." I watched as she walked to her car, a white BMW with a GO REBELS! school bumper sticker near its rear license plate. Sara Fife was nice. And gracious. Okay, the Crimson Maidens thing still made me cringe. But clearly that was only one small part of who she was. I had to face it: I'd only seen Sara's negative qualities because that's all that I'd wanted to see, so that I could go for her guy. Lillith had been wrong. It turned out the Sorority Queen Exception didn't apply to Sara Fife at all.

18

The next day, I told Jack about my close encounter of the Sara kind at Starbucks, conveniently leaving out the part where she called him her first love. I said how nice she'd been, how she'd offered me her friendship. It made him helium-balloon happy, even more than the fact that at the event the night before, his mother hadn't said a word about their fight. If Sara Fife had come around, Jack said, it meant everyone else would, too.

Jack's words proved prophetic. It was as if Sara was a CEO who had signed off on liking Kate, so now it was company policy. Everyone was friendly to me. Crystal sat with me at lunch to say she was giving a Halloween party, would Jack and I come? Pansy Clifford, with whom I'd never before had an actual conversation, invited me and Jack to join a bunch of her friends at her family's cabin at Land Between the Lakes. At last, I had truly become a part of Jack's circle of friends, and I hadn't compromised my beliefs to do it.

I had a great talk with Lillith that night. I told her how happy I was, in love with Jack, in love with life, and finally, at least in like with Redford. I also gave her the blow-by-blow on Sally Redford v. Jensen Pride. (Her Lillith-esque response: "Your mom rocks. Now, send Mrs. Redford a little note and suggest that sexual release would do wonders for her tension.")

A month earlier, if someone had told me that I'd have fun at a party thrown by Crystal Evans, I would have asked that person what they were smoking. And if they'd told me that Sara Fife would loan me an antebellum dress (complete with hoop petticoat) so that I could attend as Scarlett O'Hara to Jack's Rhett Butler, I would have been deeply concerned for their mental health. But both of those things happened, and Halloween night was one of the best times I'd ever had in my life.

Compliments of Crystal's parents, there was even a hayride. A farmer drove up in his John Deere tractor lugging a load of hay. We all tumbled in, hay and costume pieces flying, breathless in a night as crisp as a perfect apple. Jack and I lay back in the straw, my hoop skirt sticking straight up like a funnel. Above us, a blanket of stars went on forever.

As long as I banished all thoughts of Sally Redford from my mind, life was rosy. But roses can bloom over hidden land mines—and you only find out when one blows up in your face.

• • •

I felt it the moment Jack and I walked into school on Thursday. Everything looked and sounded the same. Lockers were slamming; kids were flirting and jockeying for social position. But the air felt different, darker. I thought it had to be because of the vote on the flag, which was set for the next day. It seemed as if the JUST SAY NO and REBELS FOREVER leaflets had bred and multiplied overnight. They were everywhere—on walls, bulletin boards, and lockers.

My foreboding increased as we walked toward Miss Bright's classroom. But now it felt personal. People were definitely staring at us, as if through some distorting fish-eye lens. "Something's wrong," I told Jack.

"Naw," he drawled, looping an arm around my shoulders. "You worry too much."

Maybe. But when he called a friendly greeting across the hall to the girl who was stage-managing *Living in Sunshine,* she pointedly turned her back. "I'm telling you," I repeated, "something is wrong."

We stopped at his locker to stash some books, then continued down the hallway. Outside the main office stood Principal McSorley, scanning faces. His eyes lit on us. "Miss

Pride, I'd like to see you in my office," he said. "Jack, please get to your first-period class."

When I was eleven, we took a family trip to France. I remember that I felt nauseous when we passed through French customs, as if the officials would think I'd done something wrong, even though I hadn't. I felt the same way now.

But that was ridiculous. I refused to give in to Dread of Authority Figure Syndrome. "It's okay, I'll see you later," I assured Jack with a smile. Then I followed Mr. McSorley into his office. He sat behind a battered oak desk. On the wall was a framed photo of him with the governor of Tennessee and a four-year-old plaque naming him Middle Tennessee Principal of the Year.

He nodded me into a hard-backed chair, then sighed. "I hardly know what to say. I've supported open debate on Friday's vote. I encourage the students of this school to freely express themselves. But you, Miss Pride, have crossed the line."

I had zero idea what he was talking about. Which is exactly what I told him.

He looked disgusted. "We both know that's a lie."

I was getting mad, which felt a lot better than giving in to terror. "No, Mr. McSorley. One of us doesn't know anything. So why don't you fill one of us in?"

With a forefinger he pushed some papers in my direction across his desk. "I'm going to leave you alone for a few minutes with this. I want you to give some serious thought to the harm you've done to this school. And then I'd like to hear what you believe would be an appropriate punishment."

I didn't hear him leave. Because I was too busy gaping at the title page of something I had never seen before in my life.

BLACK AND WHITE AND REDFORD ALL OVER

A new play by Kate Pride

ACT ONE

SCENE 1

A drama class at Redford High School in the small town of Redford, Tennessee. Drama teacher MISS DULL *stands before her class. She has Tourette's syndrome and has body jerks, facial tics, and uncontrollable hand movements. Kids laugh at her behind her back.*

MISS DULL: *(ticcing wildly)* Soon we will be voting on whether the Confederate flag should remain the emblem of Redford High, so we'll do an improvisation to help get you in touch with your feelings on the issue. Let's all close our eyes. Now, you are the flag. *Be* the flag. You're waving in the breeze—

The bell rings. Kids gather up their stuff to head out.

MISS DULL: Excellent work! Remember play practice after school. If you don't work on my wonderful, fabulous play, you flunk!

Students and Miss Dull exit. Three students stay behind: TIA,

CINDY, and DAN; all good-looking, popular, the in crowd that rules Redford High.

TIA: "Be the flag?" She is such a loser.

DAN: I'm surprised some black kid didn't go, *(imitating someone illiterate)* "Miz Dull, I ain't gonna beez no racist flag."

CINDY: *(imitating both Miss Dull's voice and tics)* Students who find this assignment offensive can pretend to be an African American flag: stupid and on welfare.

They all laugh together in a mean way.

DAN: They just want free handouts from white people.

TIA: Because they're all lazy and on welfare.

DAN: Right. No matter how much we give them, they want more.

CINDY: Maybe we should burn a cross on someone's front lawn.

DAN: I'd do it if I thought I could get away with it.

TIA: Well, what are we supposed to do, just let them take over our school?

CINDY: We don't have to worry about that. Kids at this school are such sheep. *Baa-a-a.* We rule this school. We tell the sheep how to vote, and we win.

TIA: You're right, Cindy.

DAN: Yes. I agree.

TIA: After we win, I'm going to tell them: We won, you lost. So you and all your low-life, agitating, boon-coon buddies can kiss my lily-white Confederate flag–waving ass.

Sick to my stomach, I basically quit reading, though the scene went on for several pages in the same ugly vein. God. Everyone must have seen it. That's why people were acting so weird. I thought of Jack. Would he think for even a moment that I'd written it?

I whirled toward the door the moment Mr. McSorley came back to his office. "This is some kind of . . . of sick joke. I did not write this!"

"Frankly, Miss Pride, I don't believe you." He sat heavily behind his desk.

"Mr. McSorley, whoever wrote this doesn't know what they're doing. It's not even in correct play form. Plus, the writing is terrible. Why would I do something like that?"

"You're the only one who can answer that, Miss Pride. I'm certain you didn't want copies floating all over the school just yet—I suppose you planned to spring the entire work on us at some point—but someone beat you to the punch."

"That's not true," I insisted.

He gave me a jaundiced look. "This school has a strict code against hate speech. In my book, what you wrote merits immediate suspension."

"You can't suspend me for something I didn't do."

Anger flashed in his eyes. "This is not a court of law. It's my school, and I'll decide how to proceed. Now, I'm going to call your—"

There was a discreet rap on his door. It opened. Sara Fife stuck her head in. "I'm sorry to interrupt, sir. But I heard you brought Kate Pride in here, and I really do need to speak with you. About her play."

He motioned her in. My hands clenched into twin fists of rage, realizing that this incident could easily ruin our new friendship. I held the stapled pages out to her, praying that she'd believe what I was about to say. "Sara, I did not write this."

"I know that," she said calmly. "That's why I'm here."

I exhaled with relief. Mr. McSorley looked momentarily thrown. He rubbed one eyebrow. "Okay, Sara, have a seat. Let's hash this thing out."

She did. Then she talked for five minutes straight, recounting some of our conversation at Starbucks and backing up my claim. "Mr. McSorley, I know for a fact that Kate has been interviewing people on both sides of the issue.

She's trying to be open-minded. I respect that. Kate and I may have had our differences in the past. But I don't believe she wrote this."

Mr. McSorley's lips were pressed into a thin line. He bounced a pencil on his desk while we waited. "Okay," he said finally. "The jury is still out on this thing. I have to do some investigating, then we'll take this up again. Both of you, get to first period."

"Yes, sir," Sara said as we both stood up. "Thanks for listening."

We left the office. When we reached the hall, I realized I was shaking. Sara lightly touched my shoulder. "You okay?"

"No." I took a ragged breath. "Thank you for what you just did."

She shrugged. "It was the right thing to do."

I smiled gratefully. "Do you have any idea who—"

She shook her head. "Someone who hates you. Well, I'd better get going."

I thanked her again and we took off in opposite directions. My feet carried me to Miss Bright's room; I felt as if I was about to face the guillotine. When I pushed through the door, Miss Bright was midlecture. "In commedia dell'arte, the actor uses movement to—"

The moment Miss Bright saw me, she stopped and plastered her fluttering hands against her sides, as if willing herself not to wrap them around my neck. I looked at my classmates. Everyone was staring daggers at me. And then my eyes found Jack's. He was gazing at me with such love and solidarity. He gave me strength. I realized I didn't have to act guilty if I wasn't guilty. "Miss Bright, may I please say something?"

"No, Kate, you may not," she replied. "I believe you've disrupted this class enough already. Now take your seat or leave. I really don't care which."

I made the endless twenty-five-foot walk to my desk. As I did, I saw copies of "my" play on desks and sticking out of backpacks. Everyone had read it. And they all loathed me for it.

Miss Bright resumed her lecture. For the rest of the period I sat stone-faced, staring at the ring I wore on the thumb of my right hand. Silver, with a tiny diamond chip, I'd inherited it from my father's mother, Gramma Rose. She had really loved me. I reminded myself that lots of people loved me. My parents. Portia. Lillith. And Jack.

"Kate?"

I looked up. Nikki stood by my desk, backpack slung over one shoulder. Next to her was Jack. "The bell rang," he said.

"I can't think of a good reason to move."

"Well, we can sit with you," Nikki offered. "Or we can blow this pop stand."

I stood. "So, today pretty much sucks."

"We pretty much know," Nikki acknowledged.

"I can't believe . . . I just can't believe . . ." I couldn't get the words out.

Jack ran his knuckles softly over my cheek. "No one who really knows you could ever believe you wrote that thing, Kate."

I felt pathetically grateful. Or maybe just plain pathetic. I hugged him. Then I hugged Nikki. Then I hugged him again. Over his shoulder I could see kids gawking through the open door.

"We could make this a three-way hug and really give them something to talk about," Nikki suggested.

I dredged up a weak laugh. Then our trio headed out to face the storm.

19

Whoever had set me up had been diabolical. There had been hundreds of copies of "my" scene distributed around school before anyone arrived, and the scene had been written so that to anyone but the most anarchic of the pierced-punk battalion, I'd be an instant pariah. Even those against the flag decided that I was an outsider who'd branded Redford with my poison pen. Jack and Nikki tried to convince people it wasn't my doing, but few believed them.

Throughout the day, Jack demonstrated his boundless optimism. He assured me this was nothing more than the high school *scandale du jour,* and that tomorrow or the next day it would be—as it always was—on to the next. Even when his friends froze him out, his spirits stayed high; he was sure it wouldn't last.

But his optimism couldn't shield me from the anonymous calls that started the moment I got home. Sometimes they came one after another, sometimes a half hour would pass before the next one. There were different voices, male and female, all well disguised. "We don't want your kind in Redford." "I hope you rot in hell, bitch."

My parents phoned the police, who told us they'd run some extra patrols past our home and advised us to turn off the ringer on the phone.

For obvious reasons, I had trouble sleeping that night. Two o'clock in the morning found me at the kitchen table, taking solace in peanut butter cookies and my dog-eared copy of *The Crucible.* It seemed like appropriate reading material: My peers had pronounced me guilty and were ready to hang me for something I hadn't done.

"Couldn't sleep, huh?"

I looked up. My mom stood in the doorway, wrapped in her favorite, oldest bathrobe. I nodded, feeling about five years old. She came and hugged me. I wished her strength would seep into me through that ratty robe of hers. But it didn't. Too soon, she let me go.

"Want some milk?" she asked. I said I did. She poured us glasses, handed me one, and sat down. "At the risk of understatement, Kate, I know this is tough for you."

"I worked so hard to get Jack's friends to accept me. And they finally did. Even Sara. Now it's ruined."

"Maybe you'll be able to use all this in the play you're *actually* writing."

"What play? I haven't written one decent scene yet."

"You will."

"Ha. It's November, and all I can do is interview people for some stupid thing I can't actually write. Not that it matters," I added with a bitter laugh. "What's the point?"

"Listen to me, sweetie. These are small-town, small-minded people. And frankly, I don't think they're going to change anytime soon." She pinched the spot between her eyes where her headaches began. "I honestly believed that moving here as a family would be the best thing for us. But I was wrong. Portia's fine, I'm fine, and it was the best thing for your dad. But it wasn't the best thing for you."

"I don't blame you, Mom, if that's what you think—"

"I know you don't. But your dad and I have discussed what I'm about to tell you. We're in complete agreement. I'm calling Lillith's parents in the morning. If they okay it, and I'm sure they will, you can go home. You can live with them and go back to Englecliff High. And I'll call Marcus, too, and try to get you back into Showcase. You haven't missed much time, really."

Two thoughts slammed into my brain at the same time: One was: a lifeline. The other I said aloud: "I'd have to leave Jack."

She regarded me for a moment. "Did I ever tell you that I once did an internship at *Newsweek*?"

"No."

"Right out of college. I had all these plans. I was going

to be an investigative journalist and change the world. I used to carry around *All the President's Men*, the book about the Watergate scandal, like a Bible."

"I thought you always wrote . . . well, what you write."

She gave me an arch look. "'*Sex Tips of the Supermodels*'? Hardly."

"So what happened?"

"I could say life happened. I got married. Had you. Had Portia. But those are just excuses. Turned out the world was not holding its breath waiting for me to become the next Bob Woodward. Writing fluff, though, came easily to me. I took the path of least resistance."

"Are you sorry?"

"Only when I let myself think about it," she said lightly, "which doesn't happen too often." She leaned toward me. "Listen to me, Kate. You are a better writer than I will ever be. You have a gift."

"You're the only one who thinks so."

"I *know* so. You can't let these people, or your relationship with Jack, sidetrack you."

"From what? Whether or not I write the stupid play?"

Her eyes searched mine. "Do you have any idea how common it is for girls to let love consume their life? All the passion that should go into their dreams and their futures goes into loving some guy."

"That's not what I'm doing!" A lump rose in my throat. "God, why do I always have to prove myself to you?"

She looked surprised. "Is that what you think?"

"Jack's mother hates me. His friends hate me. Complete *strangers* hate me. And it hurts, okay? That's all I know right now. It hurts."

"Oh, Kate." She reached for me again, and rocked me like she hadn't since I was a little girl who still believed my mother had the ability to make everything okay. "It's going to be fine, honey. You'll go home. You'll be happy again."

I sat back and fisted the tears from my cheeks. "You really think I should go home?"

"Absolutely. And sweetie? If you never wrote another word, I'd still be proud of you. Night, Kate. Try to get some sleep."

"Night, Mom."

I didn't get any sleep. Instead, I sat at the table until the sun rose, thinking about what she'd said. If I went back to Englecliff, I'd get my life back. But there'd be no Jack. If I stayed in Redford, I'd have Jack. But there'd be no life.

20

It was only a few hours later when Jack picked me up for school. He looked squeaky clean and shiny; I looked as bedraggled as I felt. But he just held me close and said everything would be all right. I wanted to believe him so much.

When we parked and got out of the car, we heard the commotion; the sounds of chanting and rhythmic clapping. But we couldn't understand what was being said until we'd rounded the corner and the main entrance was in view.

R-E-B-E-L
THAT'S OUR REDFORD REBEL YELL

R-E-B-E-L
IF YOU DON'T LIKE IT GO TO HELL!

At least a hundred students were gathered at the flagpole, chanting in unison. Their leader led them from atop the flag's base, bullhorn in one hand and Confederate flag in the other. It was none other than Jared Boose.

R-E-B-E-L
IF YOU DON'T LIKE IT GO TO HELL!

We watched as more kids streamed toward the flagpole. "Why isn't anyone stopping them?" I wondered.

"Freedom of speech comes to mind," Jack said.

"Hey, y'all," Nikki called cheerfully as she stepped over to us. "So, just another fun morning in Redford."

I was surprised by her breezy attitude. "You're not upset?"

She waved a dismissive hand. "They can holler and hold their breath until they turn Confederate gray and it still won't change a thing. We have the votes, they're going down, and they know it. You are looking at their last hurrah."

A couple of TV camera crews pushed through the crowd as the protesters started chanting Jared's name. "Ja-red! Ja-red! Ja-red!"

"I'm surprised it's not Chaz up there," Nikki told Jack. "Or one of your other buds."

"Come on, Nikki. I mean, I know they acted ugly yesterday—I'm not making any excuses, but—"

"You are too," Nikki insisted.

"You don't see any of them with Jared now, do you?" Jack challenged.

"That's because Jared has the IQ of a turnip and they don't want to be seen with him. But you can bet a whole lot of your friends agree with every word that boy is saying."

Before Jack could respond, Jared's amplified voice boomed out over the crowd. "Attention, everyone. Y'all listen up! I'm Jared Boose, I'm a senior, and I'm a straight-up Rebel man! We got us an important petition, and I'm fixin' to read it to y'all."

His girlfriend, Sandy, handed him a clipboard. "'We students of Redford High believe the Rebels and the Confederate battle flag should remain the proud and mighty symbols of Redford High School. We are the South. Let us wave our pride!'" The R-E-B-E-L chant went up again, forcing Jared to shout. "And the thing is, we already got almost two hundred signatures! All y'all, come on and sign up. Don't let 'em steal our school!"

"R-E-B-E-L! R-E-B-E-L!" But as people pressed forward to sign, a different chant erupted from a knot of kids near the old Civil War cannons.

NO JUSTICE, NO PEACE!
NO JUSTICE, NO PEACE!

NO JUSTICE, NO PEACE!
NO JUSTICE, NO PEACE!

Veins bulging in his neck, a clenched fist thrust skyward, Nikki's brother Luke was leading the impromptu counter-rally. A dozen kids—mostly black, but some white—surrounded him. More were joining by the second. As one of the camera crews hurried in his direction, Luke shaped his right hand into a pistol and popped off an imaginary round at Jared.

Nikki looked disgusted. "Fool."

The shouted invectives got uglier, and the groups edged toward each other. We were caught in the middle. "Let's get out of here," Jack said.

Just then, Mr. McSorley appeared on the front steps with a bullhorn of his own, flanked by a line of teachers and administrators. He looked furious. "Attention, students! The bell has rung. Any student not in class is subject to suspension!"

Boos and jeers greeted this pronouncement. Undeterred, McSorley announced that attendance would be taken in exactly five minutes. Though Jared urged his group to hang tough, kids began to straggle into the building. With no enemy to confront, Luke's group broke up, too.

"Well, the South shall not rise again this morning, thank you very much," Nikki opined. "Let's go vote that flag into history, where it belongs."

• • •

I hesitated outside Miss Bright's class, thinking of the possible reception that awaited me. I hoped Jack was right, that *Black and White and Redford All Over* would be yesterday's news. But just in case, I avoided all eye contact on my way to my desk.

As I was about to slide into my chair, I saw the note on the seat. YOU'RE DEAD. I plucked it up. Underneath was a baby wren with a broken neck.

It wasn't over. Maybe it would never be over. Had someone killed this bird just to scare me? Who could be that cruel? From his seat, Jack couldn't see what was happening. I didn't want him to. I found some tissues, wrapped them around the bird, and gently put it in my purse. Screw them, I told myself. By Monday, I'd be back in New Jersey and they'd be nothing but a bad memory.

But what about Jack? What about Jack?

I sat, keeping my face impassive. The students who'd been aware of the note and the bird turned away, disappointed at my lack of reaction.

Miss Bright quickly took attendance, then held up a large brown envelope. The referendum had been scheduled for the start of first period so the results could be announced at the end of the day. "This is an extraordinary moment in the history of this school," she proclaimed, hands massaging the air. "As many of you know, I was a student here myself. . . . Of course, that was back when dinosaurs roamed the earth." There were a few chuckles.

"Since we moved to this building, Redford High School students have been known as the Rebels and flown the Confederate flag. Today, you students have the opportunity to change that, if you wish."

Sara's friend Pansy swiveled around to glare at me. Had she been the one to write the fake play? Had it been a whole group from right in this classroom?

"Before you vote, though," Miss Bright continued, her fluttering hands going into hula-dance overdrive, "there's something I need to say. Advanced drama has always been a family. Sadly, this year, that's not the case. There's been entirely too much divisiveness in the name of politics. As artists, we must rise above these things. I hope that however today's vote turns out, we'll all accept it and move on together as one—"

"May I have your attention, please," Mr. McSorley's voice blared over the tinny school PA system. "Attention, all students and teachers."

Miss Bright held up a wait-a-moment finger. Anticipation crackled through the room.

"As you know, the vote on our school team name and emblem was scheduled for this time," our principal continued. "But the chairman of the Redford Board of Education has just informed me that in light of this morning's unsanctioned demonstrations on school property, I must postpone the vote until we can proceed in an atmosphere free of threat and recrimination."

Vocal reactions burst forth like buckshot, obliterating whatever else the principal was saying. "Students!" Miss

Bright shouted, stabbing the air in the direction of the speaker.

". . . that the school board will meet two weeks from Monday night to discuss the issue," McSorley continued. "All are encouraged to attend. Thank you very much for your understanding. I look forward to seeing as many of you as possible at the football game this evening. That is all."

"He can't do that!" Nikki declared, her eyes aflame. Meanwhile, Pansy had a satisfied smile on her face.

Luke barked a nasty laugh. "I knew the man wasn't gonna let this go down."

"I understand that many of you are disappointed," Miss Bright allowed. "I'm sure that after the school board meets—"

"After the school board meets?" Nikki echoed, incredulous. "We're not the ones who started things this morning. But we're getting punished for it!"

"Poor Nicolette, let down by The Powers That Be," her brother jeered. He stood. "When you gonna wake up, girl?"

"I didn't give you permission to leave your seat, Luke," Miss Bright said.

"I didn't ask for it." He turned to Nikki. "Asking will *never* get you the power. You want power, you got to just *take* it." With a cold look at Miss Bright, he strode from the classroom. She made no effort to stop him.

It was clear that a commedia dell'arte lecture would be pointless, so Miss Bright decreed the period to be a silent study hall. When the bell rang, Jack and I tried to talk to Nikki, but she rushed ahead of us. By the time we got into the hallway, she was already huddled with a group of her black friends. Behind them, some guys were ripping JUST SAY NO flyers off the walls, ignoring the teachers who tried to stop them. I saw that most of the proflag posters were already gone.

"What is happening to this school?" Jack asked. "I can't believe it."

I could. We rounded the corner and reached his locker. He spun the combination. When he lifted the handle, it didn't open. He tried the combination again. Nothing. "Great. It's stuck," he pronounced. "I have to go down to the office."

We didn't get more than thirty feet before the way was blocked by a noisy crowd. We edged close enough to see Jared Boose and one of Luke's friends in a shoving match that was obviously about to turn into a fight. "You wanna piece a this, bitch?" the black kid taunted Jared, pushing his shoulders.

"Come on, big man," Jared jeered. He raised his fists.

Jack got right between them. "Y'all need to chill!"

"I don't take orders from you," the black kid sneered.

Jared let out a whoop. "Let's kick his ass, Redford!"

"Shut up, Jared," Jack snapped. "If I was inclined to kick anyone's ass, it'd be yours."

The circle of spectators oohed at the dis. Jared reddened. A moment later, a couple of teachers with walkie-talkies arrived, and the crowd broke up.

Jack and I continued to the office, where a half-dozen kids were trying to get the attention of Miss Walsh, the secretary. "One at a time!" she insisted.

A harried-looking Mr. McSorley came out of his office. When he saw Jack, he stopped dead in his tracks. "What are you doing here, son?"

"My locker's stuck," Jack explained. "But it looks like Miss Walsh is busy now. I'll come back later."

"It's not stuck. The combination was changed."

Jack was as mystified by this as I was. "Why?"

"It's not your locker anymore, Jackson. Didn't your mother talk to you?"

"No, sir. About what?"

Mr. McSorley looked physically pained. "She pulled you out of school. You start at Corinth Military Academy in Mississippi on Monday."

Jack's jaw fell. He seemed incapable of speech.

"That can't be right," I insisted. "His mother would have said something."

Mr. McSorley ignored me and put a hand on Jack's shoulder. "I'm sorry, Jackson. You never should have found out like this. But you'll have to take it up with your mother."

"I have your belongings, Jackson, " Miss Walsh said, her voice tremulous. She reached under the counter for a cardboard carton and handed it to him.

I looked around. Was it my imagination, or were those who'd heard the exchange gloating as they watched the king of Redford High School deposed so publicly? Jack just stood there, staring into the open box as if it held the secret to turning back time.

21

We buried the wren under the biggest magnolia tree in front of Redford House, then went inside. His mother must have anticipated our arrival. She wasn't there, but the note she'd left for him on her embossed stationery was. She wouldn't be home until late that evening, but in any event, there was nothing to discuss. She'd done what she believed was the best thing for her son. He'd start military school in Mississippi on Monday. She hoped that one day he would understand.

He sat at her desk and pressed his fingers to his forehead. "I can't believe . . . How could she . . ."

But she could. And she had. A shroud of guilt settled on

my shoulders. "If you weren't with me," I said, "she never would have done this."

He shook his head. "It's more than that. Turning down The Citadel. Applying to Juilliard . . ."

"Yeah, but she blames me for—" I stopped abruptly. An amazing thought had just flown into my brain.

Jack looked up at me. "What?"

Juilliard. New York City. Why hadn't I thought of it before?

"Jack, listen to me. Last night, my mom said I could—*should*—go home to New Jersey. Back to my old school. And she said she'd try to get me back into Showcase, and if anyone can pull that off, it's her. But I thought, No matter how much I want my life back, I can't leave Jack. That's why I haven't said anything to you about it." My words tumbled against each other. "But you see, now I don't have to leave you. Because you can come with me."

I waited a moment for the idea to sink in. The more I thought about it, the more I knew it was exactly the right solution.

"It could work, Jack, I know it could! You could finish senior year there. Or take acting classes. Or both. You could audition for Juilliard right in Manhattan. It's perfect!"

"I . . . could," he said slowly, as if trying the idea on for size.

"You have your own money—you told me so. Plus you turn eighteen in March. I don't think your mother would chase you. It'd be too humiliating."

He frowned and ran a hand through his hair. "What about my soccer kids?"

"We'll talk to Nikki. I'm sure she can find them a new coach. We can do this. We can. Don't leave me. Please, Jack. Don't leave me." I slid onto his lap and wrapped my arms around his neck, clinging to him like a life preserver. The overwhelming neediness I felt seemed to belong to another girl, one Lillith and the former me would have disdained. And yet there she was. She was me.

Jack held me for a long time. Then he touched his lips to the pulse of my wrist. And he said, "Yes."

• • •

We spent the next few hours planning. We decided he would depart that night and found a flight that left Nashville at eleven-thirty. I called an actor I knew from the Public Theater who basically lived at his girlfriend's place and arranged for Jack to stay in his apartment for a while. When Sally Redford got home, she'd find a note saying that Jack was fine and he would contact her later. I'd fly to New Jersey on Sunday. Knowing how strenuously my parents would disapprove, I wouldn't tell them Jack would be in New York too. By the time anyone figured out that we were together, it would be too late to stop us.

Jack packed a small suitcase and put it in his car; we returned to school just in time for the final bell. As kids streamed from the building, we tracked down Nikki—the only person in whom we planned to confide. She was with her boyfriend, Michael, who'd come down from Louisville for the weekend. After Nikki introduced us, I was about to tell her our news. But before I could, she came at us with hers. Michael was here to help organize a boycott of that evening's football game—they were trying to convince the black players not to play. Could we make some calls?

I forced down a wave of shame as I told her we were leaving town. Though I could see that she was hurt, she didn't try to guilt-jerk us. But she didn't want to discuss it, either. She had work to do. In the face of that, neither Jack nor I dared to ask her about helping to find a new coach for the Warren Elementary Strikers.

I could hardly believe it, though, when Jack decided to ask Chaz. Chaz, who wasn't speaking to him. But Jack refused to believe that one disagreement could erase a lifetime of "brotherhood." Plus, he didn't want to just slink off. No matter what happened, looking Chaz in the eye to say good-bye was the right thing to do.

I understood, in a way. It would be like me having a terrible fight with Lillith and then moving away without another word. I knew how much it would mean to Jack if Chaz said yes—that this wasn't a forever parting; that the ties that bound them were frayed but not torn. I wanted Jack's faith to be rewarded, so much.

We knew we could find Chaz at Jimmy Mack's with the rest of the football team, putting on the feed before the game against South Columbia High. We got there at five o'clock. The buffet line already snaked out the door. Jack took my hand, and we edged inside. The place was packed—a raucous meal presided over by Big Jimmy, who wore the world's largest Redford Rebels football jersey. We maneuvered through the crowd to the booth near the window, where Jack and his friends always sat. They were all there. Chaz. Crystal. Sara. Terry and Tisha. Joined by Pansy Clifford and a guy I didn't recognize.

"Okay, we got seven black starters," Chaz was saying. "We've been together for years. They told Nikki if they don't play, they're hurtin' their own! But the pressure's still on 'em."

"People are such sheep," Sara said, tossing her hair. "I don't think—" The moment Sara saw Jack and me, she quit talking. So did everyone else.

Be nice to him. Don't blame him. He didn't do anything. Please.

That's when I saw it. Miracle of miracles, there was empty space between Tisha and Terry, as if they'd saved us two seats. There could only be one explanation: Sara had talked to them. A rush of gratitude washed over me.

"Hey, Kate. Hey, Jackson," she said, greeting us warmly.

Jack's face stretched into a grin. "Can we get in there?" He nodded at the open seats. Terry eyed him, then edged closer to Tisha, closing the gap. As they moved, Sara's eyes caught mine, and she made a helpless gesture. Then the conversation at the table picked up again as if we didn't exist.

Jack stood there, arms dangling, unable to digest their cruelty. But cold fury washed over me. I leaned close to him so he'd hear me over the din of the restaurant. "Let's just go."

He shook me off and tapped Chaz on the shoulder. "Hey, buddy. When has my word ever not been good enough for you? You'll throw it all away over a lie about Kate?"

Chaz's face tightened. But he didn't look up.

"What about 'I got your back, man. Always'?" Jack went on. "That doesn't mean anything to you?"

"Yeah," Chaz finally said. "It means something."

"Well, all right, then." Jack held out his hand, a peace offering.

Chaz got up slowly and faced Jack. "You're the one turned on us, Jackson. You want your friends, just come on back, buddy. *Alone.*"

"That's how it is?"

"Yeah, Redford. That's how it is."

Jack nodded and lowered his hand.

• • •

As Jack and I stood outside Jimmy Mack's, he peered back at the windows as if, by force of will, he could make his friends understand. A college-age black couple passed us on the sidewalk. Suddenly, I had a flash of a moment from decades ago, one I'd heard about from some of the people who'd lived it: Eight or ten black college students, dressed as for Sunday church, were being led out of the restaurant by a pair of grim-faced cops. As they walked, they passed a gauntlet of screaming, cursing white people, some of whom were brandishing Confederate flags. Two women were trying to stop the angry crowd, but no one would listen.

"Kate?" Jack reached for my arm. "You okay?"

My cell phone rang before I could answer him. It was my mother, calling with an update: Everything was set for New Jersey. Lillith's parents would be happy to have me, and Lillith was apoplectic with joy. I'd been re-enrolled at Englecliff High. Best of all, she'd reached Marcus, who said he'd take me back in Lab *and* Showcase.

She also said that Nikki had called off the boycott of the football game. Evidently the black players didn't want to let their teammates down against arch-rival South Columbia. Instead, there'd be an antiflag rally on the courthouse square on Sunday, after church.

"Let's see, what else," my mom went on. "Portia's going to the game with Cassidy, Alan, and 'Barney-the-boy-in-her-class.' Your dad and I are driving to Nashville to see a movie."

"Have fun, Mom. And thanks for everything you did for me." I gulped. I felt awful, hiding my true intentions from her.

"Hey, that's what mothers are for. Are you sure you're okay?"

"Fine. Really." We hung up.

I wasn't fine, of course. As much as I wanted to get the hell out of Dodge, I knew that people would take my disappearing act as a sign of guilt, believing that I'd turned tail and run scared. That thought made me sick. Jersey girls don't back down from a fight when we know we're right.

Jack and I were in some weird space between gone and good-bye, so we spent the next couple of hours driving around Redford. His eyes lingered on every store, church, and landmark. We stopped at the Peace Inn to see who might be there. Just a handful of kids and one of the volunteers, who told us everyone else had gone to the football game.

Jack turned to me. "Let's go," he said impetuously.

I wasn't sure what he meant. "To the game?"

"I haven't missed one in years. We don't have any reason to hide. Neither of us did anything wrong."

Well, that was certainly true. And these last few hours in Redford meant so much to him. I couldn't say no. So we went.

22

The game against South Columbia was always a major event; this year, because there were league championship implications, Redford's stadium was packed well before kickoff. As we passed through the entrance and looked for a place to sit, we greeted so many of the people I'd come to know in my brief time in Redford. Jimmy Mack. Birdie from the Pink Teacup. Mr. Derry from the Shell station. Our garbage man, who always told me to "stay sweet" when he saw me. Our next-door neighbors from Beauregard Lane, who'd brought us banana bread the day we'd moved in.

Jack and I were making our way to some empty seats on

the thirty-yard line when we heard a kid's voice calling. "Hey, Jack! Kate! Over here!"

We turned and saw Cooper Wilson, the redheaded boy from the Strikers soccer team. He stood at the top of the bleachers, waving his hands wildly to get our attention. We waved back and made our way up to him. He looked skinnier than I'd last seen him, his skin sallow, his jeans full of holes.

"Hi," I said. Cooper gave me a bashful salute.

"Hey, buddy," Jack said, giving Cooper's shoulders a quick hug. "Who're you here with?"

"My sister Tiffany and her zit-face boyfriend. Hey, lookit." He pulled a sheet of notebook paper from his pocket and thrust it at Jack. It was a math test, with a big red A on it, and "Excellent!" scrawled in a teacher's handwriting. "'Member you helped me study for it?"

"This is great, Cooper!" Jack exclaimed. "I knew you could do it."

"I never got me no A in my life," Cooper said proudly, hitching up his pants. "My momma don't even know some of them answers." Some kids walked by, carrying slices of pizza. Cooper licked his lips. "Hey, we goin' for pizza Sunday? After we whup the Lions?"

Jack blinked quickly. "I might have to miss the game."

"Nah," Cooper insisted. "My cousin's comin' from Clarksville. I done told him all about you. His soccer team ain't even got T-shirts."

"Cooper James Wilson, don't you hear me hollerin' for

you?" His older sister loomed in the aisle about twenty feet away, hands on hips. "I said come on, we're sittin' over yonder."

Cooper rolled his eyes. "I gotta git. I'll catch you Sunday. Go Strikers!" he yelled, thrusting his fists in the air as he headed for his sister. "Go Rebels!"

Jack puffed air against his lower lip. "Damn."

"I'll find them a coach," I assured him. "My dad, maybe. It'll be okay."

Jack nodded, but he didn't look convinced as we found two seats directly on the aisle, about twenty rows up from the field. The home side of the stadium was now standing room only, and the visitors' side was rapidly filling with South Columbia fans. Most of them were black. Behind them loomed Redford Hill, with its gigantic GO REBELS logo spotlit against the darkness.

"There's your sister," Jack pointed.

I saw Portia with her friends down by the field, at the fifty-yard line. Barney sat to her right, Cassidy to her left. Cassidy's mother sat a little ways down from the foursome. My sister was facing Barney, so she didn't notice me. She was laughing about something, and she whacked Barney's shoulder. I was going to miss her. A lot.

"You know, we might could fetch some groceries after the game and take them by Cooper's," Jack suggested. "Before I catch my plane."

I nodded. "Definitely."

"Warren Elementary does a big Thanksgiving pageant

every year," Jack went on. "The Strikers always say it's for sissies, but they really want to be in it. Last year Cooper was the turkey. They'll be hurt I'm not there."

"Maybe a teacher can videotape it. And explain to the kids that she's sending you the tape."

"Yeah. Good idea." Jack ran a hand through his hair. "I can't help 'em with their homework from New York, though."

"On the phone," I suggested.

He nodded. "Right, right."

Down on the field, the band marched in place as it played a brassy rendition of "Rocky Top," the University of Tennessee fight song. The cheerleaders and drill squad did their pregame routines, and the scoreboard clock ticked down the time until kickoff. Jack's eyes took it all in, memorizing each detail. "There's Mrs. Augustus and her husband," he said, nodding up the aisle.

We stood to greet the elderly couple. Her courtly husband, Alvin, who'd worn a jacket and string tie to the game, helped Mrs. Augustus along. She smiled broadly when she reached us.

"Why, hello, Jackson. And Kate. Jackson, I miss seeing you at the library."

"I'll miss you, too," Jack said. "I mean, I *do* miss you, ma'am."

"I just ordered some wonderful new plays," she continued. "August Wilson's latest. And a new book on Method acting I thought you'd enjoy."

"Thank you, ma'am," Jack said.

"And Kate? How's that play of yours coming?"

I had a difficult time looking her in the eye. "I've been thinking that I may not be the right person to write it. I feel like I'd have to live here for a few lifetimes first."

"I can understand that. But don't give up, Kate." She took my hand between hers. "I ordered something for you, too. A videotape of a play by Anna Deveare Smith. *Fires in the Mirror.* Do you know it?"

"Her name sounds familiar."

"Well, I think you'll find her work very provocative. Now, I want both of you to come in and see me soon."

Jack barely nodded; I said something noncommittal. Mrs. Augustus lingered a moment, as if there was more she wanted to say. But in the end she just said her good-byes and continued down the aisle with her husband.

Jack put his head in his hands for what felt like a long time. When he looked at me again, his eyes were anguished. "Kate, do you know that I see you everywhere? I smell your perfume on the wind. Hear your voice in my head. I'm so much more *myself* with you. To be without you would be . . . but I can't . . ."

He stopped, searching for the right words. Tentacles of fear curled around my windpipe. Because I already knew.

"I can't go with you," Jack continued. "It's not just that I'd be walking out on Redford. I'd be walking out on the person I want to be. But I don't want to lose you, Kate."

Have you ever known a boy who could say such a thing

and mean it with his whole heart? Me neither. Before Jack, that is. Now, I already understood that you can't always get what you want in life. But at that moment in the football stadium behind Redford High School, I learned that sometimes there's a moment when your highest self shows you how to get what you need.

Instead of hurling myself at Jack's feet to grovel, to beg, this peaceful feeling came over me. Instead of closing down, something inside of me opened up.

"You won't," I said, surprised at the firmness in my voice, at how right this felt. "Because I'm not leaving Redford."

He looked confused. "After the way they've treated you—"

"Jack, if I go, I'll never find out who set me up. These people will never learn how wrong they are about me. I'll never write the play I want to write, and they'll never see it. And Nikki—I should stay and help her fight. And . . . well, that's enough right there."

"What about Lab? And Showcase?"

"That hurts," I acknowledged. "But they'll be there next year, I hope. Besides, I know who the best person is to take over your team. Me."

"You'd do that?"

"Well, I was thinking we could kind of do it together. Corinth isn't that far away. You can come home on weekends so we can see each other, and you can coach their games. I'll do your tutoring. Once you turn eighteen, transfer back to Redford High if you want. Your mom can't stop you. I'll be right here waiting for you."

"Why would you do that?"

I shrugged. "Temporary insanity. True love. Sore loser. All of the above."

"Are you sure?"

"No. But I figure sometimes you just have to make a stand. They can't get rid of me that easily. And neither can you."

He laughed. "I think the ghost of Stonewall Jackson has occupied your brain."

"I didn't learn it from him, Jack. I learned it from you."

"You are one amazing girl, Kate Pride."

"Working on it, anyway."

He hugged me and whispered into my hair how much he loved me. I liked the me he was hugging so much more than the me who couldn't breathe without him, who was so desperate to run away from everything, and even more desperate for Jack to run away with me.

The game announcer's voice rumbled over the PA system. "Ladies and gentlemen, please give a warm Redford welcome to the South Columbia High School Barbarians!"

The South Columbia team, in daunting black uniforms with gold trim, charged out of the dressing-room tunnel. Their fans cheered, while the Redford fans booed good-naturedly. As the Barbarians jumped around near their bench, pumping themselves up, our band and cheerleaders formed a double-file corridor near the tunnel. When they were in place, the PA system again echoed off Redford Hill.

"Please welcome . . . your Redford High School Rebels!"

Pandemonium reigned as our team charged forth in their white home uniforms with red numerals and the band struck up our fight song. The cheerleaders formed a pyramid. Then Sara did an impressive tumbling run and got boosted to the top. She looked great up there, red ponytail whipping in the wind. To think that I had once misjudged her as badly as her friends were misjudging me now. Amazing how they'd all just blindly agreed that I was this horrid person. Hadn't I overheard Sara saying that people were sheep? She was so right. They'd follow some—

I gasped. Rewound my thoughts. Holy crap. It couldn't be.

"You okay?" Jack asked.

"I'm not sure."

Didn't Sara just use the same line at Jimmy Mack's that some character—Sandy? No, Cindy—had used in that poison play?

They're all such sheep.

Was it really possible that she had totally set me up? Made friends with me ahead of time, written the play, and then rushed to my defense so that no one would ever suspect she was the one who'd written it?

"Hey, you just turned whiter than the Rebels' uniforms," Jack told me. "You okay?"

I didn't answer him. My mind was going at warp speed. What had Sara said that night at Starbucks about writing? *Every time we get a creative writing assignment I just wilt.*

"You having second thoughts?" Jack guessed.

"No. Jack, how's Sara at creative writing?"

Jack looked perplexed. "Strong. She had a short story in the literary magazine last year. Why?"

She'd lied about being a weak writer just to sucker me in. Oh my God. Oh. My. God.

"Jack, she did it."

"What, you mean . . . you think she wrote that play?"

"I know she did." I jumped up and started to edge into the aisle.

"Where are you going?"

"Down to the field. To kick her ass."

Before I could move farther, though, the PA announcement boomed off Redford Hill. "Please stand and honor America as we sing our national anthem." The crowd rose as one, spilling into the aisles. I was momentarily stuck. I stood on tiptoe, peering around people, searching the sidelines for Sara.

Well into "The Star-Spangled Banner," we saw maybe ten kids run out of the dressing-room tunnel, each carrying a bunch of huge red-and-white helium balloons. "What's going on?" I asked Jack.

"Dunno," he answered.

The band kept playing; when the kids reached the field,

they let go of the balloons, which jerked skyward. As they rose, a giant Confederate battle flag unfurled. Delighted, the crowd on the Redford side roared in support.

But none of it made any sense. Because more than half of the kids who had carried that pole onto the field were black, and one of them was Luke Roberts.

"Oh, say, does that star-spangled banner . . ."

The balloons carried the Confederate flag skyward. It must have already been doused with lighter fluid, because when Luke raised a lighter to the fabric, *whoosh!* A sheet of flame enveloped the banner as it drifted out of everyone's reach, burning, burning, burning against the night.

The end of the national anthem was lost; all hell broke loose. Enraged Redford football players—Chaz leading the way—charged across the field toward Luke and his friends, who dashed for the South Columbia sideline. Practically the entire Barbarians team stepped forward to protect them. Fists flew; bodies fell. Enraged spectators leaped the fences surrounding the field as the announcer pleaded for calm. The police moved in, swinging their batons, but were immediately sucked into the melee. Suddenly, we heard a loud bang echo off Redford Hill. Someone near us bellowed, "That's a gunshot!"

People screamed, stampeding for the exits. Jack grabbed my arm as someone almost knocked me over. A crying child fell near us and we helped her up, trying to find out who she was with. A woman—her mother—grabbed her up and ran.

The aisle was now completely blocked. "Down to the field, then under the stands," Jack called over the bedlam.

We clambered over the seats in front of us. As we did, the ambulance that was always on duty at games tore across the gridiron, heading for the Redford side. It stopped near the fence by the fifty-yard line, and the paramedics jumped out with a stretcher and supplies. "Someone's hit," I said breathlessly as we leaped over another row of seats.

"Keep going," Jack urged me. "Don't stop."

I wish I'd listened to him. If I hadn't paused, it would have given me a few more precious moments of Before. Because my existence is still defined by Before and After. Before I knew who'd been shot. And after I saw that it was my little sister.

23

(five months later)

As I stood in the rear of the crowded Redford Cinema, waiting for my play to be performed, I was in the throes of my worst-ever pre–opening curtain panic attack.

The theater was almost full. I knew so many of the people in the audience. Kids and teachers from school. Principal McSorley. Members of the Redford police department. Reverand Roberts and his family. Mrs. Augustus and her husband. Even Sally Redford. No wonder I couldn't breathe.

"Hey, Kit-Kat."

I turned. My parents had just walked in. I hugged them

both tight, holding on for dear life. My father ended the embrace and held me at arm's length. "It'll be fine, Kit-Kat. I know it."

"I wish I did," I said, barely able to get the words past my cotton-dry lips.

My mother put an arm around my shoulders. "Look around, Kate. All these people, together. It's something. And you did it."

"Not really, Mom." I knew she'd understand what I meant.

"I wish Portia was here, too," she said softly. Choked up, my father nodded.

"Well, we should go sit," my mother said. "We checked in with the videographer. He's set to tape in the balcony, like you asked. Are you sure you don't want to be with us?" I'd reserved tenth-row center seats for them.

I shook my head. "Too long a run." I hitched my thumb toward the rear exit doors. "In case I need to hurl."

She smiled. "Okay, then. We'll see you afterward."

They each hugged me again before we headed for our seats. The one I'd chosen for myself was in the last row. I peeled off the *Reserved* sign I'd taped from armrest to armrest and sat down, the sign in my hands. Two beads of perspiration rolled off my forehead and plopped onto my lap.

I tried to calm my nerves by focusing on the play's set, such as it was. The movie screen itself was the backdrop. In front of it was a pair of coatracks from which hung various pieces of clothing—jackets, hats, and scarves. There was a sofa from Goodwill, my dad's Barcalounger, a table and a hard-backed chair, and the bloodstained rug from Redford House. That was it. Otherwise, the stage was bare.

"You think she needs mouth-to-mouth?" I heard Lillith ask BB. My two best friends from home had flown in that morning (a total surprise to me, arranged on the sly with my parents) and had slid into the two seats to my left.

BB scratched his chin. "My guess is, depends on who's offering. Remember, Kate. Oxygen in, carbon dioxide out. And repeat."

"You smack me with a ruler again and you're dead," I warned.

Lillith raised one newly pierced eyebrow. "You smacked her with a ruler?"

"In a very loving way," BB explained solemnly, hand over his heart.

"Acupressure?" Lillith guessed. "Voodoo? Kinky foreplay?"

He grinned lazily. "All of the above?"

"Mmm, interesting," Lillith purred.

"You two are *flirting*?" I yelped. "I'm about to spontaneously combust, and you're *flirting*?"

"Notice how it distracted you," BB pointed out.

Lillith nodded. "You're not gasping like a beached carp anymore. Which, by the way, is not your best look."

"Thank you *so* much."

BB leaned past Lillith and massaged my neck with his left hand. "Close your eyes, Kate. Visualize serenity."

Visualize serenity. Highly unlikely, considering. But I tried, knowing that BB was just trying to help. And I suppose that when two friends surprise you by flying a thousand miles, you can't really begrudge them a little flirt time.

An even bigger surprise, in some ways, had come from Marcus. When I'd arrived at the theater, a dozen long-stemmed roses had been waiting for me. The card read:

> *Good-bye, sitcom writer. Hello, playwright.*
> *Now the real work begins.*
>
> —*Marcus*

I'd mailed him a copy of my play, so I was very flattered. But honestly, I didn't think I deserved any credit. Because I hadn't really written it. In fact, I'm still not sure I should even call it mine.

I checked my watch. Five minutes past curtain time. The show could start at any moment. I exhaled as deeply as my constricted diaphragm permitted, glanced down at the program that I'd taken out of my back pocket, and reread my note to the audience.

I looked up. The lights were dimming; the audience hushed. Lillith squeezed my hand. It was time.

A HEART DIVIDED

a performance piece

created by
Kate Pride

A Note About Tonight's Performance

Not long after my family and I arrived in Tennessee, I decided to write a play about Redford High School's struggle over the Confederate battle flag. I must have started that play twenty times; each effort was a miserable failure.

I had just about given up when the one and only Mrs. Augustus invited me to the library to watch a tape of Anna Deavere Smith's Fires in the Mirror.

Fires. . . . *is about the 1991 civil disturbances in Crown Heights, Brooklyn. For her play, Ms. Smith interviewed dozens of people involved in the story—black and white, Jew and gentile, young and old—and then turned verbatim excerpts of her interviews into a performance piece. Later, when I read her script, I saw how she'd treated her subjects' words as poetry.*

Ms. Smith found truth in the words of real people, in the poetry of everyday speech. She and Mrs. Augustus inspired me to look in the same place. The piece you're about to see is the result. In her play, Ms. Smith played all the parts herself. But since I can't act, I asked two brave and talented friends if they'd perform my play. Tonight, all the female characters will be portrayed by Nikki Roberts, all the male characters by Jack Redford. They spent countless hours listening to the tapes I made, so that they could capture the voices of the characters you'll see tonight. The three of us worked together on the physical selves and body language I observed during the interviews.

I want to thank so many people, especially those I interviewed for a play I was never able to write but who allowed me to use their words here. And most of all, I want to thank Mrs. Agnes Augustus and Ms. Anna Deavere Smith.

I dedicate this play to my sister, Portia.

A HEART DIVIDED

Compiled, edited, and directed by Kate Pride

All female characters—Nikki Roberts
All male characters—Jack Redford

CHARACTERS IN ORDER OF APPEARANCE:

KATE PRIDE (*Redford High School Student*) .... NOW I KNOW
DR. ANTHONY BLASI, JR. (*Sociology Professor*) .... POLYVALENT
JEREMY EPPS (*High School Student*). . TEN WORDS ABOUT THE SOUTH
DR. BO ALFORD (*Historian*) .... HALLOWED GROUND
LUKE ROBERTS (*R.H.S. Student*) ..... WHAT INTEGRATION MEANS
NIKKI ROBERTS (*R.H.S. Student*) .... THE STUDENTS SHOULD VOTE
CHAZ MARTIN, JR. (*R.H.S. Student*) .... AMERICA
JACK REDFORD (*R.H.S. Student*) .... CHOOSE
REV. LUCAS ROBERTS (*Pastor*) 1961
CHRIS SULLIVAN (*Editor*) .... ALL THINGS CONFEDERATE
REV. FRED TAYLOR (*Political Organizer*) .... A LONG HAUL
MRS. AGNES AUGUSTUS (*Librarian*) .... JIMMY MACK'S
RON BINGHAM (*Plumber*) .... WITH GOD AS OUR DEFENDER
MALIK EL BAZ (*Lawyer*) .... NEVER BOW DOWN
NIKKI ROBERTS (*R.H.S. Student*) .... THE DAY OF THE VOTE
PAUL MCSORLEY (*R.H.S. Principal*) .... WE MAY NEVER KNOW
LUKE ROBERTS (*R.H.S. Student*) .... HOW THEY DO
JARED BOOSE (*R.H.S. Student*) .... TALL, COLD LADIES
PETE PRIDE (*Design Engineer*) .... I REMEMBER
DR. KARLA EPSTEIN (*Trauma Surgeon*) .... WOUND BALLISTICS
PORTIA PRIDE (*Sixth-Grade Student*) .... THIS MAGIC 8 BALL
JACK REDFORD (*R.H.S. Student*) .... THE FAMILY BIBLE
NIKKI ROBERTS (*R.H.S. Student*) AS IF GOD WAS HOLDING HIS BREATH
KATE PRIDE (*R.H.S. Student*) .... A HEART DIVIDED

Kate Pride *(Redford High School Student)*

I'm sitting on the window seat in my bedroom, speaking into a small dictation-style recorder. I'm a seventeen-year-old junior at Redford High School. I have brown hair with auburn streaks from the sun, brownish-goldish eyes; I am slender but not skinny, medium height. I'm wearing ancient, ratty sweats. My family moved to Redford from New Jersey a few months ago.

Now I Know

I've wanted to be a playwright
since I was twelve years old.
So when Marcus, the playwright
who taught my writing workshop, said:
"Your plays are as shallow as sitcoms,"
it just really hurt.
Like someone telling a proud mother that her baby
  is ugly.

I wanted to write a play
about Redford High's Confederate flag controversy.
I thought:
"This will prove to Marcus that I'm a serious writer."
He always used to say:
"You can't write what you don't know."
Well, I'm this Jersey girl, right?

I *knew* I didn't know.
So I started interviewing people who did.

Which was fascinating.
But it didn't help.
Everything I wrote was awful.
Really, really awful.
So I thought:
"Well, maybe Marcus was right.
Maybe I write shallow because I *am* shallow.
Maybe I'll never be more than a shallow writer."
And I just—I hated feeling that way.

It's funny. Ironic, I mean.
It wasn't until my own life
and my own family
became part of the story
that I finally understood:
I couldn't write it, because I hadn't lived it.
And I could never tell it as well
as the people who had.

What I learned is:
how it feels to love so passionately you can't even breathe
and
how it feels to hurt deeper than the bone and
that good really can come from tragedy and
if I could

I'd still give up all the good
to undo the tragedy.

What I learned is:
I am *not* a shallow person and
if I live long enough inside the truth,
someday—I hope—I'll be able to write it.
Because I can honestly say:
Now I know.

Dr. Anthony Blasi, Jr.

(Professor of Sociology)

Dr. Blasi teaches sociology at Tennessee State University, an historically African American university in Nashville. Dr. Blasi, slightly smallish, sees the world through thick glasses and from under long brown-with-gray hair that is tied back in a ponytail. No longer trim, he still looks younger than his fifty-seven years. He wears multipocketed khaki pants and a blue patterned sports shirt. We meet in his cramped office at TSU, where he has to move some papers off a chair for me to sit.

Polyvalent

Symbols can be polyvalent.
Multivalued.
People will rally
around a symbol,
but often for different reasons.
You take the
American flag,
being waved so much now.
For some
it refers to a simple
group feeling
that they feel threatened,
And they want to reaffirm to others
that it's

a representation
of civil liberties.
And for others,
it's for everyday life
that's being disrupted.
So people will take a flag,
but affix
different meanings
to it.
People will rally around a flag,
and not around the meanings.
Intellectuals get worked up
about the meanings,
but oftentimes people are more
upset by the burning of a flag
than by the reason why
it's burned.

Jeremy Epps *(High School Student)*

Jeremy Epps is a tenth grader from McMinnville, Tennessee. I meet him at the food court at the mall when he and his girlfriend ask me what I'm writing. Jeremy is medium height, thin, with sandy hair and a strong Tennessee accent. He wears an army T-shirt and baggy jeans. When he finishes high school, he plans to join the army. He was shy at first but got more comfortable when he spoke about his family.

Ten Words About the South

I'm gonna be kinda famous for being in your story?
The first ten words that come to mind
when I'm asked about the South:
Hot.
Fun.
Boring.
I'm trying to think—
Weird.
Twisted.
It can be Exciting.
Deep. There are deep people around here.
Wild.
Redneck.
Girls.

Mama was born in California,
so she's not really from the South.

But she's lived here most of her life.
And Daddy's a Rebel.
He's been in the South his whole life.
He's all about the Rebel flag.
I mean, that's just his heritage.
My grandmother,
she's just a regular sweet old lady.
That flag is just a flag to her,
it's just the Southern flag.
None of that racism stuff bothers her.

Dr. Bo Alford
(Curator, Battle of Redford Museum)

Dr. Alford is the curator of the Battle of Redford Museum. He's in his fifties and has a long, angular face. We meet at dawn on the dew-covered battlefield, now the municipal golf course. Near us, clumps of golfers stand around, waiting to tee off.

Hallowed Ground

We are walking today on
Hallowed Ground.
Back in 1863—
on this very earth—
in the space of three hours—
almost five thousand men died horrible deaths.

Major General Redford was *here.*
(he points to the grass under our feet)
And the Union lines were *there.*
(he points toward the far end of the first hole)

Two Confederate charges
nearly wilted the Federal lines.
Redford tried to persuade his superiors
to remain on the offensive.
But a timely Union strike
at the Rebel left flank

forced the Army of Tennessee
from the field of battle.

The land was littered
with casualties on both sides.
There was no morphine for the wounded.
There were no paramedics.
Only death on
Hallowed Ground.

Today they play golf on
Hallowed Ground.
There is a fast-food restaurant on
Hallowed Ground.

I had a great-great-grandfather in that battle.
He opposed secession
but fought for the South.
I had another great-great-grandfather
who owned slaves—I'm not proud to say.
Both men died in that battle.

People don't know.
People don't realize.
One out of every three Southern
white men of military age
died
in the Civil War.

One out of every ten up North.
Today, half of white Southerners
are descended from Confederates.

Northerners need to think—
to imagine—
a war fought in
Newark.
Chicago.
Detroit.
For Southerners
the war was fought
on a thousand battlefields
beneath our very feet
where the blood of our fathers
fed
the roots of trees
that even now
stand
on Hallowed Ground.

Luke Matthew Roberts *(R.H.S. Student)*

Luke is a senior at Redford High. A straight-A student, he has elected to attend Fisk University in Nashville—a traditionally black school—rather than Harvard. Both schools offered him scholarships. Luke is tall, slender, and muscular under his baggy clothes. He taps a foot or drums his fingers impatiently throughout our conversation at the Taco Bell in Redford, and speaks in staccato bursts.

What Integration Means

My father is a preacher.
He raised us on the
Integration Hallelujah.
(imitating his father)
WE ARE *ALL* EQUAL IN *GOD'S* SIGHT!
WE MUST *LIVE TOGETHER* IN A BEAUTIFUL
RAINBOW
CAN I GET AN AMEN?

My parents think holding hands and singing "We Shall Overcome" will defeat racism.
Shee-it.
You think white teachers
treat a gifted brother
like they
treat a gifted white boy?
Nah.

Goes against integration's
assumption of stupidity.

Integration means
Brother's suspected of everything.
Integration means
Brother didn't earn it,
somebody gave it to him.
It means
Brother's guilty until proven innocent.
Stupid until proven smart.
That's the Holy Grail,
unholy lie,
called Integration.

Institutionalized insecurity.
Internalized inferiority.
Integration gave us Redford.

Nicolette Michelle Roberts
(R.H.S. Student)

She prefers to be called Nikki. She's a senior at Redford High School, Luke Roberts's twin sister, and Reverend Roberts's daughter. She is tall and slender and moves with the grace of a dancer. Like her father, she is a motivator of people. Next year she'll attend George Washington University in Washington, D.C. She plans to enter politics. We sit in the bleachers at Redford High during our lunch break. There's a lot of background noise from PE classes and the like.

The Students Should Vote

Our parents raised us to be color-
  blind.
I had black friends,
white friends,
whatever.

It wasn't until I was in middle school
that I realized:
Everyone at our church was black.
And my white friends went to white
  churches.

It wasn't until I was in middle school
that things changed:

Some black friends accused me of "acting
white."
Some white friends stopped inviting me over.

It wasn't until I was in high school
that I got really angry
that the Confederate flag
was the emblem of my school.
That our football team
was called the Rebels.
Those symbols
didn't represent me.
Those symbols
didn't represent a lot of people.

People said:
"Redford High's emblem has
always been the Confederate flag.
The football team
has always been the Rebels."
I said:
"Wrong.
Only since 1961.
When my daddy
led the sit-in at Jimmy Mack's.
Before that,
it was the Wranglers."
People can be so ignorant.

They don't even know
the history of their own town.

I thought the students
should have a chance to vote—
did we want a new team name?
A new school emblem?

The principal said
we had to gather student signatures and
if we got enough signatures
we could have our vote.
He gave us an impossible job,
and we did it.

We must have made thousands of flyers:
JUST SAY NO to the Confederate flag.
More and more students got behind it.
It was gratifying to see how social action
was leading to real change.
We knew we had the numbers.
We were going to win.

Charles "Chaz" Martin, Jr.

(R.H.S. Student)

Chaz is a senior at Redford High who will attend The Citadel next year, as his father and grandfather did before him. He has dark hair and eyes, a broad chest, and a friendly grin. He plays tight end for the Rebels football team. We sit on his front porch, in rocking chairs. His tone is straightforward and earnest.

America

I was raised to be proud
of my Southern heritage.
I'm not going to apologize for that.
Heritage.
Tradition.
These things are important.
They tell you who you are in the world—
where you belong.

It is real hurtful when people assume that
if you have a high esteem for the
Confederate flag
you must be a racist.

I think slavery was evil.
It's always evil
for one people to enslave another people.

But it goes back to the Bible.
Blacks aren't the only ones
who have been slaves.

I plan to enter the military
to serve my country.
I will be proud to do so.
And if my country
sends me to war
I will go.
I would give my life
to defend the United States of America.
Not white America.
All of America.
Where we believe in liberty and justice for *all.*

Jackson Redford III *(R.H.S. Student)*

Jack, eighteen, is a senior at Redford High School. The town is named after his great-great-grandfather, Major General Jackson Redford, a hero of the Civil War Battle of Redford. We're in Jack's home, the historic landmark Redford House. An heirloom rug stained with Major General Redford's blood lies on the floor. Jack is as classically handsome as the general for whom he was named. When he's nervous, he runs his hand through his hair.

Choose

My family and friends
have very strong feelings
about the Confederate flag.
For them, it's a symbol
of history,
honor,
tradition.
But I know that other people
look at that same symbol and see
prejudice,
racism,
slavery.
And, I mean,
it's exactly the same symbol.
I guess if one side is right
then the other side must be wrong.

I don't think that,
but that's what people think.
So they invest all this energy
into fighting over it
and to me it just seems—I always thought—
what does it accomplish?

Once—I was little—
I asked my mother why there was evil.
I have no idea where that came from.
Darth Vader maybe.
(he laughs self-consciously)
And my father walked into the kitchen—
I can see him there with the coffeepot in his hand—
my father said:
"So there can be good."
(a long pause)
Don't know how I got off on that
or what it has to do with—
(he pauses and runs his hand through his hair)
There are kids
right here in Redford
that go to bed hungry every night.
White kids.
Black kids.
Every other color kids.
We have homelessness here.
We have poverty.

And you know, that's evil.
And I feel like if—
if half the energy
that went into fighting over that flag
went into doing something—
doing good—
(he pauses again)
A hungry kid
doesn't care about that flag.
He just cares that he's hungry.

Reverend Lucas Roberts

(Pastor, Columbia Pike Baptist Church)

Reverend Roberts is fifty-nine but looks younger. He's not a large man, but his presence and voice are powerful. He was an army chaplain in Vietnam and was very involved in the civil rights movement of the 1960s. We're in the rear pew of his church in the late afternoon. He's wearing a dark suit and tie. Sunlight streams through a window and dances across his crisp white shirt.

1961

My father was a preacher man right here in Redford,
so you could say I went into the family business.

An incident that stays in my mind
occurred in the summer
of 1954.
Blacks—they called us Negroes then—
weren't allowed
in the municipal swimming pool.
One night—one of those steamy ones—
my friends and I decided to sneak into that pool.
That cool water felt so *good.*
We got caught, but
we managed to get away.
The next day,
they drained the entire pool.

(his hands are clasped; he shakes his head at the memory)
Nn-nn-nn.
Can you imagine such a thing?
They thought three black children had
contaminated
the water.

In 1961 I was a freshman at Fisk University.
I looked up to the older students
who were fighting segregation.
Wanted to roll with the big dogs.
So I joined
the sit-ins
at Woolworth's in Nashville.
Blacks were not allowed to sit at the lunch counter.
The segregationists fought us mightily.
A group of white teenagers attacked us.
Our morality of nonviolence
dictated that we would not fight back and
we did not.
Yet we were arrested and
the white boys went free.

In court the judge turned his back
on our attorney, Z. Alexander Looby.
That judge *literally* turned to the wall
during our defense.
Then Mr. Looby's home was dynamited.

Momma wanted to drag me home after that
but Daddy said: "Leave the boy be."

The next day
we held a silent protest march
more than two thousand strong—
black *and* white—to city hall.
And my father marched by my side.

When we arrived
Mayor Ben West
told the marchers and
the city of Nashville and
the South and
the United States of America
that it was immoral
to discriminate against a person
on the basis of race or color.
Six weeks later
those lunch counters
were integrated.

I guess I had proved myself, and
after that
some of the older students said to me:
"What's the name of that restaurant
in Redford you told us about?"
And I said:

"Jimmy Mack's."
And they said:
"Lucas, it should be next."
And that is how the fight for equality
came to Redford.

(he pauses, his brow furrows)

Good people. Righteous people—
black *and* white—
shed their blood
for the rights of the black man
to be served like any other customer
at places like Jimmy Mack's.
And now,
all these years later,
my own son hates that place.
He and his friends
go to Taco Bell.

Christopher Sullivan
(Editor, Southern Partisan *magazine)*

I speak by phone to Mr. Sullivan in his office in South Carolina, but saw him in a videotape about the Confederate flag created by the First Amendment Center in Nashville, so I know he is in his mid-forties, of medium build, with a trim beard and glasses. When I ask what he's wearing, his answer is precise: a tweed jacket, white shirt, blue-and-yellow striped tie, navy pants, brown shoes recently polished. He speaks passionately. On the tape I saw, he often karate-chopped the air to emphasize a point.

All Things Confederate

The key to understanding
the argument over the battle flag
is really an argument
over what the flag means.
If you say that the flag is
bad
or
evil
or
there is something
wrong
with it
because of its meaning—
whatever bad meaning is attached to it—

well then,
logically,
there's something
bad
or
evil
about the monuments, too.
Something
bad
or
evil
about those
who served under that flag.

And so
if you agree with those premises
and you say the logical result
of that argument is that the battle flag
has to be removed from public places,
then those monuments
should be removed from public places.
It's inescapable.

To say: "We've got to get rid of the battle flag"
is to say:
"We've got to get rid of all things Confederate."
And that's something that most Southerners—
and a lot of Northerners—
are not prepared to accept.

Reverend Frederick Douglass Taylor

(Political Organizer, Southern Christian Leadership Conference)

Fred Taylor is the coordinator of direct action for the SCLC, the Atlanta-based civil rights organization founded by activists including the late Dr. Martin Luther King, Jr., in 1957. I interviewed him by telephone. He spoke slowly, his words gaining passion as the interview continued until they achieved a sermon-like cadence. From what he told me, I know that Mr. Taylor is in his sixties, bearded, bespectacled, and balding. From a photo I saw of him, I know that he has a huge smile.

A Long Haul

I was thirteen years old
living in Montgomery, Alabama,
at the time of the Montgomery bus boycott.
I have a Movement history.
When I came here in '69,
I mean, I was full of optimism.
I thought I had joined in a process—
or Movement—
that was going to change—
we were going to change the world.

But as time moved on
I discovered that has not happened.

The struggle now, it is, it is,
it is insidious,
it is computerized,
it is not as obvious as it once was.
We are in for a long haul.

What has surprised me most
in the struggle over the battle flag
is that the sons and daughters of the Confederacy
believe in maintaining those symbols
to the degree that they have
invoked a theological undergirding
for their position.
They really believe that
their position
is ordained by some
Divine Power.
They are so *entrenched* and so *fixed*
in their position
that there is no reason for compromise.
It is either
their way
or no way
at all.

But by taking down,
taking away these symbols,
it would take away

divisiveness
and usher in an era of
inclusion
and coming toward the day
when, as Dr. King often talked about—
when people
would be judged by the
content of their character
rather than of the
color of their skin.

The proper place
for the battle flag in twenty-first-century America,
in my opinion,
is in some museum of the South,
for persons who have the need to preserve that.

I don't think the battle flag
ought to fly over any public facility.
But if there are
private facilities,
or in a Confederate cemetery,
or a war memorial,
I don't have any problem
or strong feeling about that.

I am an eternal optimist—
that's why I'm still here,

doing interviews with you,
and speaking in schools,
and participating in demonstrations,
and going to jail every now and then,
and making my witness.
But in terms of bringing about
the kind of
beloved community
that Dr. King talked about
we are still in for a long haul.

Agnes Augustus
(Librarian, Redford Public Library)

Mrs. Augustus, eighty-four, has a halo of white hair, a peaches-and-cream complexion, and piercing blue eyes. Wearing a flowery dress and sensible shoes, she is slender and has excellent posture. Her manner is both forthright and feminine. We meet at the Pink Teacup over fruit tea and chocolate-chip cookies. The drawl in Mrs. Augustus's voice is soothing. Soft classical music plays in the background.

Jimmy Mack's

When I was your parents' age
there were signs posted everywhere:
Whites Only.
Colored Drinking Fountain.
Blacks couldn't stay at most hotels
or eat at most restaurants.
There were laws about it.
It was a way to make blacks second-class
citizens.
And not just in the South.

You know Jimmy Mack's restaurant?
It was whites only till 1961.
Back then, Lucas Roberts was a student at Fisk.
He and nine other students

walked right through the front door of Jimmy
    Mack's.
The boys wore jackets and ties.
The girls wore lovely dresses.
They took seats at two tables
and waited.

All the white people were served.
But these ten young people were ignored.
So they sat there all day
in silence.

At the end of the day
these young students came outside to find
white folks
lined up on the sidewalk.
Cursing them
and
waving the Confederate battle flag.
I tried to get them to stop.
So did Birdie's mother.
But they wouldn't listen.
(she looks sad and sips her tea)

I know this will be difficult for you to understand.
I still love that flag.
I used to fly that flag from my front porch
with great pride.

It was the banner of the soldiers, not the Confederacy.

My grandfather died in battle under that flag.

So did Birdie's ancestor—

The one who freed his own slave.

But after that day at Jimmy Mack's

I brought it inside.

I haven't flown it since.

Ronald Bingham *(Plumber)*

Mr. Bingham is forty-four, medium height with a slight build, just starting to bald. We're at his small frame home in Pulaski, Tennessee. He's just come from a plumbing job and still wears work clothes, boots, and a UT Volunteers baseball cap. From the next room I can hear the voices of his two small children, as well as the voices of the cartoons they're watching, throughout the interview.

With God As Our Defender

They try to say that
the Confederate Flag
is a flag of racists.
You know.
The Mud People,
Queer Nation,
Communists,
The Children of Satan Jews
who control the media.
The godless.
The mongrelized.
There's a lot of them out there.

We dare say aloud what
others only think. We say:
"Rebels! Be proud. Stand tall! We are the South!"

Do you understand what these people want?
They say they want to
take down our flag.
But what they really want
is an end to their own white race,
and you can take that to the bank.
Do you know what was
the motto
of the Confederate States of America?
Deo Vindice.
With God as our Defender.
This was the Confederate motto.
This is the motto we live by today.
Make no mistake about it.
The white Anglo-Saxons
are the *true* Israelites.
We will smite the enemies
of God's chosen people and
then the world shall be returned
to our righteous hands.

Malik El Baz *(Attorney, Political Activist)*

We speak in his office in north Nashville, where he has a criminal law practice. Mr. El Baz appears to be in his thirties. He's tall, with sinewy arms visible beneath the rolled-up sleeves of his black shirt. A loosened tie dangles from his collar. Behind him on the wall are photographs of Malcolm X and the deceased Kenyan leader Jomo Kenyatta. He speaks emphatically but at the same time seems in complete control.

Never Bow Down

If any racist
straw-chewin'
tobacco-chewin'
racist redneck
lays their hands on any righteous
black man or black woman
who is the flower of humanity—
my people should *crush* that devil
who is trying to do them
harm and evil.
In the Name of God
and in accordance
with their legal rights.
(he stops and folds his arms)

The state of Israel—
it's causing problems

all over the earth
for people of color.
We will never bow down to the
white Jewish Zionist onslaught.
I say to all Jewish people:
Stop pushing your Holocaust
down my throat.
Stop your cover-up of the worst Holocaust
humanity has ever seen
perpetrated by *you* against *my* people.

That flag?
That racist, disgusting, cracker
loser of a flag?
Burn, baby, burn.

Nikki Roberts *(R.H.S. Student)*

(As before)

The Day of the Vote

What happened was,
the day of the vote,
a lowlife brain-dead white boy
staged a demonstration
in front of the school
in support of the flag.
In reaction,
another group,
which unfortunately
was led by my brother Luke,
began demonstrating against them.
Which I thought was misplaced energy—
because we were going to win.

The principal
used the demonstrations
as an excuse
to cancel the vote.
He said it was "postponed."
(she sneers and shakes her head)
It wasn't until that day
that I really *got* racism.

That I truly understood:
The ones with the power
will do almost *anything*
to hold on to that power.
(she looks at me with steely resolve)
Let them underestimate me.
That's fine.
Because I am my father's daughter.
I will *never* give up.
I will *never* give in.

Paul McSorley

(Principal, Redford High School)

We meet in his office immediately after school. His desk is covered in papers. There are photos and awards on the wall behind him. Kids' voices can be heard in the hallway. Mr. McSorley is a paunchy fifty-one. He has a gray crew cut and wears a plaid sport coat with an American flag pin.

We May Never Know

I taught American history for fifteen years
before becoming principal.
I've put twenty-five years of my life
into public education.
I *willingly* scheduled the flag vote—
at some peril to my professional
    standing—
because I believed
it was the right thing to do.
What did I get for that?
Disruptive demonstrations
in front of my school
that very nearly turned into a riot.

I believe in freedom of speech,
but the *safety* of my students comes first—

especially in this day and age.
I perceived the situation that morning
to be potentially very dangerous.
That is why I immediately informed
the Board of Education,
and why the vote was postponed.
I've been accused
in print and on TV and Lord knows
what-all
of canceling the vote.
I *postponed* the vote.
And I stand by my judgment.
This is my school.
The buck stops right here.
*(he jabs a forefinger on his desk for
emphasis)*

Never in my twenty-five years
as an educator have
I seen anything as terrible
as what happened
before that football game.
But the media barely mentioned
that of the eleven—
the people on the field
who burned
the Rebel flag that night—
Of eleven, only *six* were my students.

Do you know that there
are twenty-four amateur videos
of the brawl and
not a single one
shows the shot being fired?
Not a one.

Lord knows what the shooter was
really aiming at.
Certainly not your sister.
We may never know.
It was just a tragic accident.
Tragic.
It fell upon me to decide
what the consequences should be
for the Redford students
who participated in this.
The only fair thing in my book
was to mete out equal justice.
The six students
who burned the flag
as well as
the six football players
who led the charge onto the field
were all expelled.
(he stops, sighs, drums his fingers on the desk)
They were mostly starters,

so that ended our season
right there.
There are still folks
who want to run me
out of town on a rail
for that.

Luke Roberts *(R.H.S. Student)*

(As before)

How They Do

My friend's aunt wears a maid's uniform.
She cooks for the Redfords
and serves their food.
She calls Sally Redford *(he clears his throat),* "Mrs.
Redford."
Calls Jack Redford *(he clears his throat),* "Mr. Jack."
They call her "Dora."
I said:
"Tell them to call you Mrs. Washington."
She said:
"Go on, boy. That's just how they do."
She doesn't mind
'long as they pay her good
and treat her good and
she ain't *about* to risk gettin' fired.

When we burned that flag
we were saying:
"We don't care
how you do
and we don't care
about the risk.

We refuse
to stand
in your bread line
for the crumbs of power."

I got my nose broken.
James got thirty stitches.
My boy Malcolm got a concussion.
That boy is fierce—yo,
he plays for the Rebels—but
when some white jock
grabbed me
and some other white jock
bashed in my face
Malcolm pulled them off me.
He chose his real boys, you know what I'm saying?
We knew there'd be a fight.
The crackers who jumped us
took their hits—believe *that.*
But what happened after—
your sister getting shot—
(he rubs his face, obviously upset)
I have a sister, too. So I can imagine. . . .

I'll tell you this:
It was a white boy pulled that cop's gun.
No doubt.
A brother might murder

for drugs or money—
which too often occurs because
he feels so put down and used up
that he commits
suicide by homicide
though he doesn't recognize it as such.
But no brother
steals a gun from a white cop
and shoots it into a crowd
of innocent people
with other white cops
swarming all over the place.
No brother is that big a fool.
Think about it.
If a brother had actually done it
he'd already have been lynched for it.
Hell, a brother'll
probably get lynched for it anyway.
Cuz you know
that's just how they do.

Jared Boose *(R.H.S. Student)*

Jared is a senior at Redford High. He's average height, very thin, with a narrow face and darting eyes. He wears a jean jacket and a backward Confederate flag baseball cap. We're in the stadium bleachers. He points to various locations as he narrates his version of events for me. It's a blustery afternoon, and he moves around a lot to stay warm. He has a strong Tennessee mountain twang.

Tall, Cold Ladies

Me and Sandy
had a big-ass blowout that night.
I stopped to pick up a six-pack
and she wants a brew and
I'm all:
"You know you ain't supposed to drink when you're
pregnant, girl."
So
she gets all pissy and pulls out her smokes.
So
I grab 'em and throw 'em out the window.
I'm all like: "You're gonna be a momma.
You gotta be more responsible."
So she just went off—
Went off.
How I ain't her daddy and I don't tell her what to do.

The girl's slapping me and cussing me out and
I'm all: "Damn, girl, get off me!"
I seen it was still early.
So
I drop her ass off at the game
and tell her I need to go
blow off some steam,
you know what I'm saying?
So I drive around for a while—
crank up my man Travis Tritt.
Just me and my tall, cold ladies
getting me a nice buzz.

Then I head back.
I find my girl,
we patch things up,
and shortly after that the preshow commences.
And well.
You know what happened after that.

What gets me is how
everyone gets theirs in America.
Blacks, women, Mexicans, or whatever.
But come up white and poor . . .
Like my daddy.
He worked over to the shower curtain factory for twenty
    years.
Company up and moves to Mexico

an'
just like that
my daddy's out of a job.
Ain't no one reaching into the goody basket for me and
mine.
That flag—
That flag says F you to all y'all.
And them people set fire to it?
And what?
I'm supposed to sit there
with my thumb up my ass
and take it?
So, hell yes
I jumped that fence
to defend my flag.
And I'd do it again.
So, I'm right in it—*BAM! BAM! BAM!*
*(he makes a fist and mimes throwing hard
punches)*
I seen this big black guy—
ain't never seen him before—
I seen him pull that cop's gun.

They hauled all of us
down to the po-lice station
and I done told them what I just told you
and they said:
"Jared Boose, you're drunk,"

and they book my ass!
Said I got me an agenda and
no one else collaborated [*sic*] my story.
They don't do squat.
I mean
I'm just some
pissant Joe-dirt white-trash redneck, right?
My word don't mean diddly.
Cuz you know that's just how they do.

Pete Pride *(Automotive Design Engineer)*

Mr. Pride is forty-five. He is of medium height; his brown hair is thinning. He has kind eyes. This interview takes place a month after the shooting. We're in the family room. He's sitting in his favorite chair, a Barcalounger, with the leg rest raised. He grew up in New Jersey and sounds like it. He's my father.

I Remember

Your mom and I
had gone to see a French film
in Nashville that night.
Things were kind of crazy at home.
I remember
you were having a really rough time,
Kit-Kat.
Someone had written a vile play
and stuck your name on it
and people believed you had written it.
I remember you got
death threats.
I wanted to—
I felt like I should—
A dad is supposed
to protect his daughter.
Daughters.

So your mom and I talked and
we decided you could go home
to Englecliff to finish your junior year.
So that was the plan.
I remember
your little sister—
A friend's mom was shlepping these kids
to the football game, and
I remember
before Porsche left we were talking—
She didn't want you to leave
because she'd miss you too much.
But she didn't want you to stay
and suffer either, which is just so . . .
(he stops and rubs his face)

Thank God I forgot to turn off my cell in the
movie.
You called and I walked outside and
you told me that Portia had been—
That something terrible had happened
at the football game.
And I had to tell your mom
and we had to get to the hospital.
I don't remember driving.
I mean I must have,
but I don't remember.
You and Jack

were in the waiting room.
Someone came out to tell us—
to say Portia was in surgery and
it was serious and
the bullet had shattered.

I remember
the hospital—
They were really good about
keeping the media and everyone away
from us,
but they let in Sally Redford.
She came with the best of intentions—
that was clear to me—
to ask what she could do to help.
And your mom got right in her face
and said—
I remember this exactly—
she said: "Your town did this. *Your* town."
(he stops, looks off, sighs)

The night before,
Porsche had a nightmare.
She asked me to check her room for monsters.
She still did that sometimes.
So I checked—you know—
under her bed and in her closet
just like when she was a little girl.

And I remember
sitting at the hospital thinking that
she'd never again believe that her daddy
could keep away the monsters.

Dr. Karla Epstein *(Trauma Surgeon)*

Dr. Epstein is a trauma surgeon at Williamson–Redford County Medical Center. We meet in the noisy hospital cafeteria. Dr. Epstein is forty-eight, with a full face free of cosmetics, surrounded by curly dark hair tied at the nape of her neck. She wears hospital scrubs, drinks black coffee, and speaks matter-of-factly. Her beeper goes off many times during our talk.

Wound Ballistics

I specialize in wound ballistics,
which is the science
of the motion of projectiles.
Your sister was struck by a nine-millimeter
    round
fired from a Smith & Wesson
standard-issue law-enforcement sidearm.

How badly you are hurt by a gunshot
has to do with the mathematics
of wound ballistics.
Um. For example.
Low-velocity bullets,
like those from handguns,
do their damage by
crushing tissue.

Your sister was shot at a distance of approximately fifty
 yards—
we're able to ascertain that by
examination of the scene, the bullet's trajectory,
and the wound itself—
which allowed much of the kinetic
energy of the bullet to dissipate.
She was fortunate
in that her body was
turned toward the boy next to her
(she illustrates by sliding sideways in the chair)
at the moment of the bullet's impact,
so the bullet entered this way,
(she uses her right hand to gesture to her right side, then swivels back to me)
which is what probably saved her life.

When the round fragmented
inside her body,
a fairly large piece
lodged against upper lumbar disc L-3,
causing it to bruise,
putting pressure on her spinal cord,
and resulting in significant
spinal cord injury.
I was able to fix the internal damage
from the passage of the bullet.
But where the fragment had lodged,

cutting could do more harm than good.
So that's why I didn't remove it.
Which is why we didn't know
if your sister would ever walk again.

Portia Pride *(Sixth-Grade Student)*

Portia is twelve, a sixth grader at Redford West Middle School. She has long brown hair, enormous brown eyes, and dimples and is extremely articulate. She is my sister. It is three months after the shooting. We're in a small room on the first floor of our house. It was probably once a maid's room, but now it's hers, so that she doesn't have to climb stairs. She walks in with the aid of two metal canes with supports that wrap around her wrists. She has an apple in her mouth that she just got from the kitchen. She settles on her bed, the canes next to her, and chomps on the apple as we talk.

This Magic 8 Ball

A long time ago Lillith told me—
Wait.
Are they going to know who Lillith is?
You should say
she's your best friend from Englecliff
so it'll make sense.
Okay—anyway—so.
Lillith had this Magic 8 Ball—
like a fortune-telling thingie?
You shake it up and your fortune appears.
So she told me
every person's fortune was in there.
Which isn't even logical.

For one thing,
what language would the fortunes be in?
I was only—really little—because I kind of believed her.
Not really, but kind of?
I asked when I would get my first boyfriend.
So she shook it up
but she didn't let me see what it said.
But *she* said it said:
"You will get your first boyfriend when you are twenty-seven."
That didn't seem right.
Twenty-seven is *old.*
So I asked you
and *you* said she was definitely wrong and
you were absolutely certain
I'd have boyfriends sooner than twenty-seven.
Like probably around fourteen.

Then it turned out
I didn't have to wait that long
because I was only twelve
when I started liking Barney
and he started liking me back.
Wait.
You need to say that I'm twelve and a half now.
Am I messing this up?
Could you say that
even though Barney has a stupid name

he's nice and cute and smart and
looks like a boy who would have a cool name
like Trevor or something?
Okay. So.
Me and Cassidy and
Alan and Barney
were going to the football game.
Last time I sat between Cassidy and her mom?
But I didn't know what to do this time.
I wanted to ask you
how we should sit.
Like
should we sit girl-girl-boy-boy,
or boy-girl-boy-girl?
But you weren't home
so I couldn't ask you.
So then we got to the game.
I sat between Barney and Cassidy,
so it turned out we were boy-girl-girl-boy.
And all I was thinking about was
if we were sitting right.
I don't remember after that.
Like
the getting shot part.
And I don't remember
the first few days at the hospital, either.
Everyone there was nice.
I liked all the flowers and presents.

At first I didn't like physical therapy
because it hurt
but then it got better.
Sometimes it still hurts but not too much.

What else?
Being in a wheelchair was bad.
Not being able to walk—that was bad.
But then after my other surgery
I tried and tried and
then I could kind of walk with these canes,
which is *much* better.
Um . . . not being upstairs
in my real bedroom is bad, too.
Also it was very difficult
trying to catch back up
with my class at school,
but I did it.
None of my friends stopped being my friends.
That was a good thing.
Oh, wait, the *best* thing is
Barney already invited me
to the spring dance
even though it's still
a month and a half away.
I am *soooo* excited
because it'll be my first dance.
The doctors say if I work

really really hard
I could be down to one cane by then,
which is *excellent*!
You'll take me dress shopping, right?
Because
when you're not wearing jeans
you have excellent taste in clothes.
And um . . . did I say enough
or do you need more?

Jack Redford *(R.H.S. Student)*

(as before)

The Family Bible

Once, Nikki said to me:
"In this town, the name Redford
is almost as powerful as that flag."
Meaning—from her point of view—
that I needed to step up to the plate.
That I had a certain responsibility
which I had been unwilling to accept.

At the hospital—
when your sister was in surgery—
I was thinking about that and
I felt—
I wondered if things
might've been different
if I'd tried to find a solution.
Instead of just,
you know,
rationalizing why
I was above the fray
or whatever.

When my mother
came to the hospital—

that took guts.
She had to know
your mom
wouldn't want to see her.
But she came anyway
because it was
the right thing to do.

You know how sometimes
in a crisis
you pick up on something completely
irrelevant?
Well, for some reason
I noticed
the emergency room nurse's little
plastic—
(he touches his chest near his heart)
you know, name plate.
Brenda Partridge.
And the trauma unit social worker's
little name plate.
Samantha Evans.
Everyone who worked there wore them.
But this maintenance worker—
janitor—
I went to the vending machines
and he was emptying the trash and
he had one of those little name plates
but his just said

Roland.
And this orderly pushing a laundry cart—
his just said
Marvin.
I don't know why it struck me.
But it did.

Hours later, Portia got out of surgery
but they wouldn't let us into intensive care.
You and I decided to go to my house
to shower and eat.
Our family Bible
was on the kitchen counter,
which was odd.
It was open to Matthew, chapter five—
"Blessed are the peacemakers,"
which I later found out
was because my mother
had been praying for your sister.
But it was almost like it was meant
to be.

On some level
I was—I guess I was thinking about—
you know—
those hospital name plates.
Because I opened to the back of the Bible,
where we keep the family genealogy.

And there were all these
old bills of purchase.
1855.
Amanda. Age 38. Black in complexion.
Samuel. Her son. Age 4.
1856.
Ginny.
1857.
Frankie.
Big Joe.
Louis. Of a hearty constitution.
Amanda. Excellent for breeding.
And what struck me—
what took my breath away was:
None of them had a last name.

But it wasn't like the—
the low-level hospital workers
because
at least their full names were known.
These people that my family *owned*—
their Africans names
had been *ripped* from them.
Their freedom
and their heritage *stolen.*
And we talk about
how people trample on *our* heritage
and look what we do—what we did—

to theirs.
We even took away their names.

So you know what happened next.
But if you want a chronology—
I guess I better
or this will make no damn sense.
So. I called Nikki.
It was—what—
four in the morning?
Her father answered.
I had to assure him
it wasn't bad news about Portia.
And he said:
"Then why in the Sam Hill
are you calling my home
at four in the morning?"
We—I think it was you—
asked Nikki to come over.
Said it was important.
When she showed up it reminded me
that
when we were kids she came over a lot
and
I really couldn't recall
when she'd stopped.

So I showed Nikki my family Bible.

The bills of sale.
The single names.
And I told her my idea—
what I wanted to do.

NIKKI ROBERTS *(R.H.S. Student)*

(As before)

AS IF GOD WAS HOLDING HIS BREATH

Jackson's big idea?
I was standing there with
the two of you and
I remembered thinking how
Jackson's house used to be
"my friend's house"
instead of
"Redford House,"
and how the only black feet
that had stepped through the front door
in years
probably belonged to the help,
and here it was,
four-whatever in the morning,
and the only reason I was there
was because
this boy
was so *thick-headed*
and *self-involved*
that *he* thought
I should get *my* ass out of bed
and run over to *his* damn house

in the middle of the night because
he'd finally had an epiphany about the evils of slavery?

Please.

Honestly, Kate.
If it hadn't been for you
I would have said—
I just would have gone off on him.
But there was so much pain
in your eyes,
and you two had been at the hospital
all night.
Plus, I knew he was well-intentioned.
So that's why I went along
with what Jack wanted to do.

The three of us wrote down
the names
of every slave
owned by Major General Redford
at the time of the Civil War.
Thick black letters on
big white file cards.
Then we went to the monument
in the courthouse square.
And we taped
all those slave names to it.

Fifty-seven of them.

(she has a faraway look, as if seeing this in her mind's eye)

That monument.

Floodlit against the streaks of dawn.

That shimmering checkerboard of

gray granite squares

etched with the names

of Union and Confederate soldiers,

and white paper ones

with our handwritten names of slaves

that weren't really their names at all.

It was so quiet.

As if God was holding His breath.

It wasn't enough.

It wasn't nearly enough.

But it was *something.*

Kate Pride *(R.H.S. Student)*

I made important changes to this monologue on the same day that A Heart Divided *was to be performed at the Redford Cinema. The actress was kind enough to incorporate these last-minute revisions. I recorded both the original monologue and the late changes while sitting on the window seat in my room.*

A Heart Divided

"A house divided against itself
cannot stand.
I believe this government
cannot endure permanently
half slave
and half free."

In case you slept through American
  history,
Abraham Lincoln said that.
Lately, I've been thinking a lot
about a *heart* divided.
How the heart of Redford
was so divided
by that monument
and the high school
so divided
by the Confederate flag.

The funny thing is,
I've been thinking
that it's okay.
Mostly.
I mean, it's the people who only want one
opinion—
their opinion—
that we have to worry about.
And then one day
an innocent girl
ends up in the line of fire.
And no one saw who did it.
And both sides blame each other.

Well, I figure the crazies on both sides did it.
Hate was responsible.

Life can be just so—
so random.
I mean, what sin was my sister paying for?
There's no logic.
No fairness to it.
Terrible things happen to wonderful people.
The only way
I can deal with
the horror of random *bad*
is to see that—from it—
we can choose purposeful good.

And we did.
Choose.

Redford High
voted
to change the school emblem
to the Liberty Bell,
and our team name to the Liberty.
The Redford city council
voted to add the names
of all the slaves
who resided in Redford County
at the start of the Civil War
to the town square monument.
Four thousand three hundred and eighty-four
slave names
now etched
forever
in the granite,
alongside the names of soldiers from both
sides.
The single slave names—
AMANDA
SAMUEL
BIG JOE—
help remind us of all
that was taken from them.
All that they lost.

And today,
the American flag
at that monument
flies three feet above
the Confederate battle flag.
To remind us.
It's not a perfect solution.
But I'm pretty sure that perfect doesn't exist.

This morning,
I noticed the
tulips in our yard
are in full bloom.
Spring is here.
The school year is almost over.
And when it is,
my family will move back to New Jersey.
My amazing little sister
will be in a rehab program
at Mount Sinai Hospital in New York.
She had her third—and hopefully last—
surgery ten days ago.
Then, yesterday, she spiked a fever.
Her doctors said it isn't serious,
but they wouldn't let her out of the hospital
for this performance, and
if you know Portia
you know how mad that made her.

We're making her a videotape.
She said she plans
to interview people
and make her own play
from the patient's point of view.
Knowing her, she'll do it, too.

Strange to think that
soon I'll be back at my old high school.
Back with my old friends.
Old house.
Old life.

You'd think I'd be *happy* to leave Redford.
And I *am* happy to leave some of it.
I'm happy to leave the football stadium,
where I still see Portia's blood.
And I'm happy to leave
the person who signed my name to a play full of hate,
and the people who were so eager to believe I was the
author.
I confronted the girl who was responsible.
She denied she'd written it,
said I didn't have any proof.
But I could see the truth in her eyes,
and she knew I knew.
Word got around.
It was a subtle thing,

but people began moving away from her.
She wasn't even nominated for prom queen.

All that—
I will be happy
to leave behind.

But then I recall
how the Tennessee breeze
smells after a thunderstorm.
The view of lush, rolling hills
from the water tower.
The taste of hot cobbler
with cold ice cream.
The hoot of a whippoorwill.
The kindness of strangers
after Portia was shot—
how they kept on being there
for weeks and
months and
as long as we needed them.
In my mind
I hear the voices of
the people who welcomed me—
the kids at Warren Elementary.
The volunteers at the Peace Inn.
Birdie
and

Mr. Derry
and
Reverend Roberts.
The amazing Mrs. Augustus
And Nikki,
who, that very first day,
put her hand out
to a know-it-all
Jersey girl
with a bad attitude.

And Jack.
He will be at Juilliard this fall.
His mother is not happy about this.
She's not happy that we're still together, either.
But she loves him anyway.
That,
I have learned,
is what mothers do.
People say that high school love never lasts.
People are wrong.

Of all the things that Redford is to me,
most of all,
it is—will always be—
Jack's hometown.
This is where I met him and
this is the place he loves and

this is the place where *I* learned to love
so passionately I couldn't even breathe.
And what it feels like
to hurt to the bone.
My writing teacher, Marcus,
told me,
"You can't write what you don't know."
Well, now you've seen the play
I finally wrote.
Judge for yourself.

A long time ago,
my mother
embroidered a pillow for me
that says:
THE PURPOSE OF LIFE IS A LIFE OF PURPOSE.
I thought
the purpose of my life
was to become a playwright.
I still want that.
But I don't think it's my *purpose* anymore.
Purpose is:
Who you touch.
How you change the world.
The good you leave behind.

I can honestly say that
when we drive away from Redford

I will look back at that monument
and see it forever changed
by the good *my sister* left behind.
And I
will be
smiling
through
my
tears.

-CURTAIN-

afterword

Redford and History

If Redford, Tennessee, were to exist, we envision it as being between the real-life towns of Brentwood and Franklin, just south of Nashville. We take liberty in making Redford a county seat; it would actually be in Williamson County. The equivalence described in Redford County between white and slave populations at the outbreak of the Civil War is similar to that in Williamson County. The bloody Civil War engagement we set in Redford is fictitious, but is inspired by the 1864 battle at Franklin, which exacted a horrifying human toll. The facts of the Nashville lunch counter sit-ins as depicted in Reverend Roberts's monologue "1961" are accurate. In

Nashville today, major city facilities are named for Z. Alexander Looby and Mayor Ben West.

A Heart Divided, *the Play*

Within Kate's play, if a character is mentioned in the narrative or is specifically tied to the internal action of the story, we wrote the monologue. If the person is someone whom Kate interviewed for context or commentary, the monologue is excerpted from a real interview that we conducted for this book. We changed some locations for dramatic purposes. We were not able to use all the actual interviews we conducted, though each was fascinating in its own right. In addition to Jeremy Epps, Professor Anthony Blasi, Christopher Sullivan, and Reverend Frederick Taylor, we thank Nashville songwriter and pastor Joel Emerson, author Don Hinkle, Tennessee river catfish guide Phil King, Charles Kimbrough of the Nashville office of the National Association for the Advancement of Colored People (NAACP), Professor Reavis Mitchel of Fisk University (Nashville), and Maggi Vaughn, poet laureate of the state of Tennessee, for their willingness to talk to us. While we gladly grant permission for classroom use of Kate's play, all other rights are reserved, including dramatic performance rights.

about the authors

Cherie Bennett and **Jeff Gottesfeld** met in 1987 when both lived in New York City. They moved to Nashville in 1990. After nearly a decade in Tennessee, they now live in Los Angeles with their son. They have collaborated on fiction, plays, and other writing projects. Bennett's *Life in the Fat Lane* was an ALA Best Book for Young Adults; their widely produced play *Anne Frank and Me* had a successful off-Broadway run. For more information, visit them at www.cheriebennett.com.